THE
TWELFTH
STONE

A Shea Baker Mystery

SALLY J. LING

ACKNOWLEDGEMENTS

Many thanks to the following individuals who assisted in the reading and editing of *The Twelfth Stone*: Pat Keeley, Judith Lombana, Rebekah Mendoza and Lisa Dykstra.

TABLE OF CONTENTS

PART I

Chapter 1

The cold dark room sprang to life as Israel's premier archeologist flipped the switch to illuminate a space the size of a modest three-bedroom apartment. Only a select few had access to the hallowed room by swiping their coded card followed by voice recognition at the main point of entry. Misha Reuben was one of them.

The chamber in which the elderly man now stood was housed in the Samuel and Saidye Bronfman Archeology Wing of the famed Israel Museum in Jerusalem, an institution that contained the most extensive collection of biblical and Holy Land artifacts in the world, including the renowned Dead Sea Scrolls. They were housed in their own climate-controlled bomb-proof underground vault.

The unannounced artifacts in this room, while quite valuable both historically and monetarily, sat on crowded shelves and in packed drawers. These archeological relics from Israel's most recent digs would remain in the room until the museum's executive director, in conjunction with high level staff and museum archeologists, decided how and when the historic objects would be displayed. Plans for exhibitions took months, even years, to execute.

Misha, who always shivered in the museum's climate controlled 72 degree temperature, drew his chunky sweater close around him and took a deep breath. The room's aroma filled his lungs with the odor of aged relics coughed up by the arid sands of time. Not that it was an unpleasant odor, at least not to Misha. To him, it was more intoxicating than a woman's perfume. The scent, which mixed with the dry coldness of modern air conditioning, seemed to merge two worlds together each at opposite ends of history.

The renowned archeologist shuffled to a massive locked steel gray vault in the corner of the room. He withdrew a ring of assorted keys from his pants pocket, selected a short silver one, and inserted it with shaking fingers into the lock. Tugging open the heavy double doors, his bright but aging eyes perused the cabinet's contents. On the three shelves of the cabinet rested eleven medium-sized wooden boxes spaced precisely one inch apart: four sat on the upper two shelves and three on the third shelf. An empty space, just big enough for one more box, appeared at the end of the row on the lower shelf.

Removing one of the wooden boxes, Misha hugged the hefty twenty-five pound container to his chest and carried it with an unsteady gait to a long aluminum-topped table. He repeated this routine numerous times. Soon, all eleven boxes sat side-by-side. A slight man, both in height and build, the archeologist's appearance belied his strength. Honed to a chiseled edge by decades of difficult archeological work, his muscles remained toned and unusually strong for his seventy-three years of age. Thankfully, the first stage of Parkinson's disease, which recently emerged as tremors in Misha's limbs and weakness in his gait even with medication, hadn't yet stolen his strength. But he knew it was waning.

The date and location where each artifact had been found were written in permanent marker on the outside of each container. The dates spanned a period of thirty-five years; the location of each discovery proved as random as the dates. Below this information was the individual who discovered the artifact. The name Misha Reuben, scribbled on each box, held this distinction.

Pertinent information regarding each boxed relic was cross-referenced in a document that resided in the museum's secure data base, and a hard copy containing a list of all recent finds, which had been disseminated to only a handful of museum staff and archeologists, sat in locked desk drawers. When the time was right, the whole world would learn of these precious relics, initiated by a timely article in the bi-monthly periodical "Biblical Archeology Today." A trade publication for archeologists, historians, antiquity dealers, and interested parties the world over, the magazine would eventually announce the Holy Land discovery while a simultaneous display of the artifacts appeared center stage in the museum's grand entrance.

Discoveries like this were what helped keep the museum alive, along with government subsidies and generous donations from wealthy patrons of the museum. In addition to this income, with the announcement of each ancient treasure thousands flocked to the museum, not unlike those who congregated at a zoo to see the latest infant panda or hippopotamus. In the wake of such crowds, revenues shot up exponentially. The display, however, had to be timed just right, when revenues needed a substantial boost.

Misha lifted the lid from the first box removed a large, smooth, irregular-shaped stone and placed it on the table with quaking hands. He twisted the stone ever so carefully and withdrew a powerful magnifying glass from a drawer. Peering through the quivering lens, he watched as the bright overhead florescent light bounced off a vague image followed by Hebrew letters lightly etched into the stone's hard surface.

He drew his fingers gently over the stone feeling for the ridges of the letters; his eyes brimmed with tears. His greatest desire was that others see the truth behind the stones. Just then, he heard the room's door open. As Misha turned toward it, disheveled white locks fell over his grey eyes surrounded by the black rim of thick bifocals.

"Ah, I see you're babysitting again." The museum's executive director, Jeff Keene, made his way to the table and stood next to the archeologist. Misha's hunched form looked like a child's next to Keene's towering six foot four inch presence.

"I can't help it," Misha said. He tucked his white lock back into place and returned his eyes to the relics. "It's taken me so long to find them."

"Patience my friend." A broad smile coupled with twinkling green eyes revealed Jeff's kind, friendly face. "It will only be a few months longer. Then the whole world will know of your discovery."

"The committee has set a date then?" Misha's bushy eyebrows shot above the rims of his glasses and his eyes scanned the director's face at this unexpected news.

"Yes. The stones will go on display nine months from now whether the twelfth stone has surfaced or not. We can't wait forever to announce the good news or add revenues to our bottom line."

"No, I suppose not." Misha's eyes and mouth took on a resigned droop at the director's response. He had hoped for a bit more time, but he couldn't blame the director. After all, his quest had taken thirty-five years. "Once people see them," he continued, "do you think they will finally believe?" The question was asked in innocent fashion, like a child querying his father, even though it was the archeologist who could have been father to the forty-seven year old director.

"I don't know," Jeff said. "There are some who have always believed, and then there are others that will never accept it no matter what you say or show them. It's an individual choice. No one can force another person to believe, despite tangible evidence."

Misha pondered his words. "It's just that now that the stones have been found, who can deny the facts?"

The question hung in the room's atmosphere like an air balloon on the cusp of losing its lift. Fact was the director didn't quite know how to answer Misha. While the distinguished archeologist had spent years uncovering the eleven stones, one was still missing. Without the final stone, the relic was incomplete not unlike an ancient mosaic mural with tiles missing from the face of the principal subject or pages torn from a book at the climax of the story. Yet, despite the missing twelfth stone, the museum decided to proceed with the display of the other stones in hopes that the world-wide notoriety might facilitate the final stone's appearance.

"It's already well after closing. Don't stay too late." Jeff gave Misha several warm pats on his back.

"No, no. I just wanted to look at them one more time before I left for the night. I'll only be a few minutes."

The director made his way to the door. "And don't forget to let the guard know when you're leaving so he can check the alarm," he called over his shoulder.

Misha rolled his eyes. He had spent thousands of late nights at the museum over the past three decades and had never forgotten this routine exit procedure. He had it down pat. Yet, the director always seemed compelled to remind him.

After the director left, Misha set the stone back in its box. Then he took the tops off all the other boxes and looked at the stones one at a time. Each was similar to the other in size, color, and shape—grey/brown flecked with white, smooth with rounded edges. A symbol was etched into each stone, similar to the first one, followed by a Hebrew word. While Misha could make out the word on each individual stone, he knew that collectively they were part of a larger message. For years, he had tried to understand just what that message was. Sometimes, he would wake in the middle of the night with a possible combination and rush down to the museum and arrange the stones in a particular order or log onto his secure home computer and place the words in a specific sequence. And while they did make some sense, he knew the phrase wasn't quite right. Without the last stone, he concluded, it would be impossible to decipher the missive. The twelfth stone alone held the key.

Misha placed the tops back onto the boxes and returned them to the vault. His shuffled steps echoed off the walls as he made his way down the tiled corridor toward the secluded employee entrance at the back of the museum. At the door, he used the house phone to announce his exit to the security guard. Once outside, he filled his lungs with the warm night air and his nostrils with the sweet fragrance of night blooming jasmine. Now that all the other employees had gone home, it was quiet, just the way he liked it, and the whiff of the nocturnal flower brought a smile to his thin lips.

He held onto the metal railing and took his time as he scuffled down several levels of steps toward his lone car parked in its designated space next to a tall hedge in the employee parking lot. As he reached his vehicle, trembling fingers pressed the button on his car key to unlock the driver's door.

"Still seeking the twelfth stone?"

Misha jumped at the deep gravelly voice that seemed to come out of nowhere. Over the top of his car, he eyed the man that now stood on the opposite side. Illumination from the overhead parking light was just enough for him to make out the man's features—in his fifties, stocky build, light stubbled beard, slicked back hair and dark eyes. His face, while handsome, had seen a lot of life and was creased well beyond its middle-aged years.

"What are you doing here?" Misha asked, recognizing the familiar face.

The men conversed in Arabic, a language Misha had come to know all too well having spent decades digging in the desert.

"Thought you might like a lead." A toothpick peeked out the side of the man's mouth.

"And you're so generous you're going to give it to me?"

"Of course," the man said, splaying his hands. "What kind of a friend would I be to withhold such valuable information?" The tooth pick bobbed up and down to the rhythm of his words.

"What do you want for it?" Misha asked.

"Money, of course. Same as the other times."

Over the years, Misha had been given many clues suggesting where the twelve stones might be. Wild goose chases—at least, some of them—four at the paid suggestion of this man. Yet, Misha didn't want to give up on any potential lead. After all, promptings from this same man had, in fact, led him to three of the other stones. The balance of the stones he had found himself through years of networking and the occasional bribe.

"Fine," Misha said. "I'll pay the same fee." He opened his car door.

"Sorry," the man said. He withdrew the toothpick with thick fingers and pointed it directly at Misha. "The fee's been raised. For this lead, you pay triple." He punctuated his last sentence with a jab from the toothpick.

"Triple?!" Misha's eyes shot the man a vile look as he slammed the car door.

The man shrugged, unfazed by Misha's loss of temper. "It's the last stone. Do you want the lead or not?"

Having spent more than half his life searching for the artifacts, Misha felt certain his own continued pursuit would uncover the twelfth stone before the magazine article came out and the unveiling of the eleven stones took place nine months from now. But . . . what if it didn't? Could he afford to pass up this possibility?

Misha gathered a breath and stared hard at the man. "Half now, half when the lead pans out."

The man returned the toothpick to his mouth. "All of it now."

"You're pretty sure of yourself."

"Sure enough," the man said. His words were as solid as the creases in his face that looked as though they were chiseled in stone.

Misha hesitated, then he opened his car door and removed his checkbook from the console. Using the roof of his car as a table, he scribbled the man a check, tore it from the book, and slid it with his fingertips toward the savvy negotiator, as if getting any closer to him would put a hex on the agreement. In exchange, the man pushed a folded piece of paper toward Misha.

"You know, you shouldn't treat me with such distain. You've benefitted greatly from my efforts, and I'm quite certain you will call on me again."

Misha shot him a "not in my lifetime" look.

After the man blended into the shapeless night, Misha opened the note like an excited child with a Hanukah gift. His eyes grew wide and his jaw dropped as he scanned the message. After reading it two more times, he carefully folded it to the size of a business card and placed it under a thin flap of leather behind the cash in his wallet. If pursuit in Israel within a reasonable length of time did not produce the prized twelfth stone before the unveiling, he would immediately jump on a plane and fly thousands of miles across the Atlantic to continue his hunt. The note told him that the stone was hidden somewhere in South Florida. Past the name of the city and that of a contact, the exact location of the precious relic was unknown.

Unknown. That word had been Misha's constant companion for the past thirty-five years. At this stage when he was so close to getting his hands on the ancient artifact, he swore nothing, not his progressively ailing body or the great unknown would thwart him from his final quest— finding the twelfth stone.

Chapter 2

Rabbi Sharon Krouse checked herself in the mirror—lipstick, eye shadow, and blush perfect. Colorful, yet not too flashy. Unruly chemically straightened strands of Sephardic curly hair at her crown were tamed by hair spray, and her dark blue suit was pressed free of wrinkles.

Today's memorial service would be difficult. Aside from the fact that Rabbi Sharon was filling in for the senior rabbi who was in Bermuda on vacation and the appearance that elderly congregants were dropping like flies—this was her fourth funeral in two weeks—the deceased, Gertrude Ginsberg, was one of the temple's most active and beloved members.

The rabbi's last gesture before she met the bereaved family was to adjust the tallit that draped about her neck—a beautiful white organza prayer shawl with gold pomegranates embroidered on it. Her long black hair flowed like an obsidian waterfall over the garment in distinct contrast to the snow white and gold of the shawl. With the Rabbi's Manual, a book of funeral invocations, held comfortably in her grasp, Rabbi Sharon took a deep breath and said a silent prayer.

Just thinking about losing Gertrude Ginsberg prompted a large tear to form at the edge of her eye. Rabbi Sharon dabbed at it with a tissue, careful not to smudge her makeup. She then stepped out of the ample changing area into the receiving room where she was to meet Gertrude's family.

"I'm so sorry for your loss." Rabbi Sharon hugged each member of Gertrude's family—one brother, a sister-in-law, and several of their grown children—who had arrived from Philadelphia for the funeral. Without any children of her own, these were Gertrude's only living relatives.

"We're just devastated. She just had her physical and aside from the usual effects of aging, she was strong. We thought she'd have at least another five to ten years." Gertrude's brother wiped his tear stained eyes with his handkerchief.

"I know how difficult this will be for you. It's also difficult for us. She was such an active member of the shul. Everybody just loved her," Rabbi Sharon said.

At 84, Gertrude's heart simply gave out, a massive heart attack the designated culprit. Joe Greene, friend and member of the temple's Visiting Committee, had stopped in to see her only minutes before and swore she was as vibrant as always and had not shown any signs of physical distress. In fact, at the time of his visit, Gertrude was baking a cake for the choir, the rehearsal of which she would attend that very evening. Known for bringing delicious baked goods to committee meetings and other gatherings, she said it was her way of giving back. When found face down in her living room hours later, Gertrude's oven was still on and the cake burned to a crisp.

At the appointed hour, the family took their seats in the first row of the large sanctuary at Temple Beth Shalom, Boca Raton's oldest and largest Jewish house of worship. At least two hundred and fifty members of the shul's congregation who came to pay homage to Gertrude's memory sat behind the grieving family.

On the bimah, an elevated platform at the front of the sanctuary, were two podiums, each at opposite ends. Rabbi Sharon would conduct the ceremony from one of the podiums while the other would be used for final words from the bereaved. Along with the podiums, a beautifully carved wooden Ark housed the sacred Torah scrolls, the first five books of the Hebrew Bible, written on parchment. On the sanctuary floor below the bimah, several poster-sized photos of Gertrude rested on easels. One photo of Gertrude showed a close up of her laughing, her blue eyes twinkling with life. In the other, she was showing friends her rendition of a moon walk. The photos were typical Gertrude—love, happiness, and joy exuding from her every pore.

Rabbi Sharon took her place behind the podium on the right.

"Let us rise and recite the 23rd Psalm." At her bidding, the mourners stood as one. A chorus of voices filled the sanctuary with a melody of verse:

The Lord is my shepherd; I shall not want. He maketh me to lie down in green pastures: he leadeth me beside the still waters. He restoreth my soul: he leadeth me in the paths of righteousness for his name sake. Yea though I walk through the shadow of the valley of death I will fear no evil. Thy rod and thy staff they comfort me. Thou preparest a table before me in the presence of mine enemies: thou anointest my head with oil; my cup runneth over. Surely goodness and mercy shall follow me all the days of my life and I will dwell in the house of the Lord forever.

The remainder of the ceremony consisted of prayers and a memorial tribute to Gertrude—her profession as a teacher, her forty-four year marriage to her late husband Irwin, her hobbies, her dedication to the temple. At the conclusion of the service, the mourners strolled down the sloping driveway to the mausoleum located on city land adjacent to the southern edge of temple property. Kaddish, a Jewish prayer praising God and expressing yearning for the establishment of God's kingdom on earth, was recited by the mourners. After the prayers, the urn, filled with Gertrude's ashes, was reverently placed into the marble niche beside that of her husband Irwin.

Rabbi Sharon concluded the ceremony with comforting words. Gertrude's family placed several smooth round pebbles on the brick floor below her niche as a sign of reverence and God's presence, then, along with the mourners, slowly dispersed. They would go to Gertrude's apartment where for three days the family would sit Shiva, a time of mourning and opportunity for the family to receive visitors.

Rabbi Sharon and Joe Greene walked side by side toward the parking lot.

"Gertrude was such a loving and giving person. It's so sad she had to leave us this way," said Rabbi Sharon, her blue eyes welling with tears for the second time.

Joe shook his head in a gesture of great sadness. "With our high percentage of elderly congregants, it could have been any one of them. This time, it simply happened to Gertrude."

"Yes," Rabbi Sharon said, "but it seems to be happening all too frequently."

Chapter 3

Professor Meyer Belinsky parked himself at his cluttered desk—a family portrait on its side atop a kinked mound of hardback text books, stackable trays overflowing with random papers, a chaotic heap of unopened mail, and an iPad that needed recharging—where he read Simone Coffee's hefty thesis. The paper, selected as a stand out by Belinsky's research assistant, emerged among dozens turned in by masters' candidates prior to the end of the semester. With the required submission, each student vied for the professor's top honor—a trip accompanying him and his wife Mary Anne to Israel to participate in an archeological dig that he arranged every summer. The one-on-one with the fifty-two-year-old professor of Jewish history was considered the pinnacle of his student's university education, and the thesis winner subsequently became a shoo-in for the doctorate program. The composition would be judged on its subject matter, depth of content, research, and, of course, presentation.

The professor propped his feet on his desk, ankles crossed. He stroked his full-faced dark beard highlighted with just a sprinkle of white as he perused Simone's paper entitled "Jewish Sands." He found it a fascinating look at one of the world's most controversial religious issues—whether Moses and the forty-year Exodus of several million Jews crossing the desert into the Promised Land had actually occurred as the Bible asserts.

Belinsky had to admit that what Simone had written conveyed a fascinating and compelling argument against the time-honored biblical story. In fact, she had included several interesting points that he had not even considered, though he, like Simone, readily discounted the entire account of Moses leading the Jews out of bondage and into the wilderness to reach the land of milk and honey, a territory promised to the "chosen people of God." After all, other than the scripture in the Bible no physical evidence or written account in a historic document had ever been uncovered to corroborate the epic event.

While the professor extolled his beliefs, better yet, the lack of them, to his students and the world through lectures, magazine articles, and numerous books—what amounted to heresy among the Jewish community—his assertions were delivered with an altruistic desire, even the compulsion, to question history in order to discover truth. Truth, he said, was the ultimate goal of research and discovery—not time-honored tradition, not fables handed down from generation to generation—no matter what kind of religious or historic wrapping they came in. He freely acknowledged, however, that today's truth shifted as precariously as dunes in the desert. Once a "new truth" reared its head out of the sands of time, especially in the Holy Land where new discoveries were almost a daily occurrence, yesterday's truth became . . . well . . . obsolete.

As Belinsky reached the end of Simone's paper, his office door flew open and slammed against the wall with a loud BOOM! The professor instinctively jumped at the disturbance and came to an immediate upright position, his chair letting out a protesting groan.

"What do you want?" His brow furrowed as his brown eyes propelled darts of enmity toward the unwelcomed intruder.

"I came to tell you the good news from the Israeli Museum," Bob Clark said in a patronizing tone. A wide smirk etched his lips as the tall lanky professor waggled in his hand a report he had just received from the renowned institution. "At least, it's good news to those of us who believe." He took several steps forward and tossed the report onto Belinisky's desk. It landed with a dull thud.

Belinsky glared at the stack of stapled papers with its yellow sticky note attached to one of the pages, then up at Clark. He wasn't about to read the report or ask what the so called "good news" was. Any good news Clark was privy to would, in no uncertain terms, not be good news to him. No . . . not under any circumstance. The two men were at direct odds with each other theologically, politically, and philosophically. Truth be told, there wasn't one thing the two agreed on despite the fact that they were the only full-time professors in the College of Jewish Studies at Florida Atlantic University in Boca Raton, Florida, and were forced to work side-by-side.

"Since you won't admit I've piqued your interest, I'll give you a brief synopsis," said Clark, the smirk still plastered on his lips. "This is a report that lists recently discovered biblical artifacts at the museum along with additional notes. The first few pages aren't that interesting, just the usual pottery shards and the like, but take a look at the fifth page, the one I've marked. Now that's where you'll find the interesting stuff. It seems as though the famed Jewish archeologist Misha Reuben has discovered eleven of the stones purportedly from the memorial erected by one member from each of the twelve tribes of Israel after they crossed the Jordan River into Canaan. His present quest is to find the twelfth stone. Apparently, each stone has a Hebrew inscription on it, and, when placed together in the correct order, Reuben believes the stones will reveal a message from God himself to the Jewish people. It's all right there in the report." Clark pointed to the papers then crossed his arms in front of him.

Belinsky wondered how Clark had gotten his hands on such a report. He knew the Israeli Museum didn't announce things this way—a list of discovered artifacts along with a narrative emailed around the world. But he had to shake that thought off. It wasn't important *how* Clark got the report; the immediate concern was that he *had* the report and what it said.

"Pity," Clark continued, "what Reuben has discovered will probably deep six your sacrilegious assertion that the Exodus never occurred and certainly unravel your career—one on which you've banked your considerable and controversial reputation. But I'll just leave you to the report and your thoughts." Clark turned on his heels and left without bothering to close the door.

Belinsky knew Clark was right. He did have quite a controversial reputation. Something the professor, and most everyone else, readily acknowledged and of which he was quite proud. Had he been employed in a setting other than a university where freedom of thought and speech was permissible, even celebrated, he knew he wouldn't be so quick to voice his opinions or enjoy such a provocative reputation. But FAU and most other universities encouraged students and faculty to question authority and challenge the policies and beliefs of government, business, and religious institutions. It was simply something ingrained in institutions of higher learning.

Case in point. Just a few years ago, FAU made national headlines when instructor Deandre Poole, who held a PhD from Howard University, asked students to write the word "Jesus" on a piece of paper, place it on the floor, and stomp on it. Course objectives for Poole's class in Intercultural Communications stated the exercise was designed to encourage students to view issues from many perspectives. When a student pushed back against the assignment, however, it created a fire storm of gargantuan proportions for the university. An immediate apology emanated from the president's office to the student, and the exercise was pulled from the curriculum. Though it was noted the professor used "bad judgment," no disciplinary action was taken against him and he retained his position. Freedom of thought and expression was the rationale, no matter how inappropriately it was expressed. Belinsky's rub against the grain of acceptability was no different than Poole's, only now with the purported discovery of the eleven stones to prove the Exodos did in fact occur, his notoriety as the university's Jewish "bad boy" could be in jeopardy.

After Clark's abrupt departure, Belinsky eagerly snatched the report from his desk and flipped to the marked page and highlighted information. If Clark spoke truth and Reuben had unearthed eleven of the twelve stones, the news would be devastating to him. And, if the famed archeologist was actively seeking the twelfth stone, Belinsky needed to find it before Reuben did. The professor's reputation, his livelihood, and even, perhaps, his life, depended on it.

PART II

Chapter 4

It was Friday morning. I was deep in the "zone" of outlining my book about the "Spear of Destiny," my last adventure of biblical proportions, when I came to an abrupt halt. I had reached a point of needing information from Tom Steele a Ku Klux Klan historian that I had recently contacted. He was supposed to email me some information for my book regarding how the organization operated in Florida. Trouble was, I hadn't heard from him. Suddenly, it dawned on me that perhaps his e-mail had landed in my spam folder.

While scrolling through my meaty junk file for Steele's correspondence, I noticed an email from Mort Saul. It was dated four days ago, marked "high importance," and the subject line read: "Urgent! Need to See You!" I made a mental note to check my spam folder more often.

A prominent businessman and devout reform Jew, Mort attended Temple Beth Shalom in Boca Raton, Florida. I had met him over ten years ago when he chaired a committee to build a mausoleum for those of the Jewish faith on city land next door to the temple, property that already included a cemetery and mausoleum for the community. After months of negotiations, the city partnered with the Temple by designating the vacant land. The Temple put up the construction money and agreed to market, manage, and maintain the facility. In exchange, the city got five percent of the sales. It seemed like a win/win for both parties.

The Jewish mausoleum was the subject of one of my articles since Jews customarily subscribed to in-ground burial—dust to dust, ashes to ashes. Because of this, Mort knew the construction of the mausoleum would take perseverance and a proactive marketing campaign to overcome centuries of tradition. Yet, Mort was unwavering in his belief that having a mausoleum next to the temple was a positive move both from a financial and public relations perspective.

"After all, what could be more convenient," he had said, "than for Temple mourners to take a short stroll from the funeral service in the temple sanctuary to the attractive mausoleum for interment of their loved one? Besides, the well-kept mausoleum with its manicured grounds would serve as a natural marketing tool to mourners who might need its services in the future."

The plan, sanctioned by the Temple's Board of Directors, had moved forward in 1995 with two phases of buildings constructed over a seven year period.

I opened Mort's email:

Shea,

I must speak with you concerning a matter of utmost importance. Please meet me at the Mausoleum at 7:00 pm Monday. Bring your camera and recorder.

Mort S

At the end of his emails were two links. The first was to a Bible passage in the Old Testament—Joshua 4:4-8—and, the other was to an article entitled "Evidence of Exodus Nonexistent."

Having followed my nose into several previous life threatening biblical adventures, ones I had turned into novels, I wasn't too anxious to get involved in another one. After all, I hadn't been in contact with Mort in many years and wondered what "of utmost importance" prompted him to get in touch with me now? And what did the scripture passage and article have to do with it? As I was contemplating these questions, Rosa, my wife of more than a quarter century, entered my home office with the morning paper.

Despite the existence of e-news, we still enjoyed getting our information the old fashioned way—sitting down over breakfast and turning pages that smudged our fingers with printer's ink. Besides, I was a former Air Force reporter who had grown up in the print news business, and although I was now retired, I steadily wrote feature articles and personal profiles for Sunshine Media, a local publisher of slick magazines. Between my former service to the military and my renewed journalism profession, I found it hard to break decades of the print news habit.

"Shea, don't you know a Mort Saul?" Rosa asked, looking up from the paper. "Wasn't he someone you interviewed a few years ago?"

"Funny you should ask," I said, "I just got an email from him."

"But . . . that's not possible." Rosa cocked her head to one side and her dark eyes questioned my sanity.

"Well, it's right here." Dull raps emanated from my monitor as I tapped it with my index finger indicating the email in question.

The color drained from Rosa's face. "But Shea . . . Mort's dead." She turned the newspaper around so I could see the headline:

MORT SAUL FOUND MURDERED IN TEMPLE BETH SHALOM'S MAUSOLEUM

My nose started twitching.

Chapter 5

Mort's funeral service was two days later. Even though we hadn't been "buddies," under the circumstances I felt obligated to attend. Plus, I wanted to understand why he had contacted me and what his message meant. I thought I might learn what this was all about if I met some of his friends, asked a few questions, and listened in on conversations of the bereaved.

I entered Temple Beth Shalom about ten minutes before the service and followed a stream of people, none of whom I recognized, down the carpeted entry. Just this side of the large wooden sanctuary doors, I signed my name in the guest book, and, out of respect for Mort and Jewish tradition, removed my felt fedora, the latest addition to my wardrobe, and donned on the crown of my head a complimentary black kippah, also known as a yarmulke. As I sat in the back of the sanctuary, hat perched on my knee, and waited for the service to begin, two things struck me. First, there were no flowers as in Christian funerals—no gladiolas, no daises, no baby's breath. Second, the steel casket was closed—no parade of mourners eyeballed Mort in his lifeless state of repose. I made a mental note of these unusual items and would ask someone about them later.

"Long time no see."

I was jolted from my musing by the deep voice of Detective Stan Warren of the Palm Beach Sheriff's Department. He slid past me and plopped down in the empty seat to my right without invitation.

"Detective," I said, giving him a slight nod of my head. Over the past few years, I had developed quite a relationship with this human bowling pin who was short, stocky, all muscle, and had a grip like a vice. It seemed whenever I got into trouble, he, or his boss, Palm Beach County Sheriff Ted Berry, managed to bail me out. Not that I was ever in jail or sought trouble, it's just that in my last two adventures, somehow trouble seemed to find me.

"You were friendly with the deceased?" he asked.

"Yes, sort of," I said, knowing from experience that every question the detective asked had an ulterior motive.

"I can't wait to hear your explanation. I'm sure it will be quite fascinating." Warren opened the funeral program and perused an outline of the service.

"Listen," I said, more than a hint of resentment in my voice, "I'm just here to pay my respects to Mort's family. That's all."

Warren chuckled. "Sure you are."

"And you? Did you know the deceased?"

"Only after he was deceased."

"So, you're here because—"

Warren didn't respond.

"Oh, that's right," I said in mock expertise, "In a murder case such as this, many times the murderer returns to the scene of the crime. I get it."

"Quiet Baker," Warren said, nudging me in the arm with his elbow. "The funeral is about to begin."

A simple and solemn service was performed by Rabbi Joseph Larkin. I had met him only once before many years ago when I interviewed him for my article on the mausoleum. A tall, stately man with brown hair and glasses, the Rabbi conducted a liturgical service and spoke eloquently of Mort's dedication to the temple, his wife, and family, and his many hours of sacrificial service to make the temple a better place in which to worship and socialize. And, of course, Rabbi Larkin spoke of Mort's unparalleled enthusiasm for the construction of the mausoleum, despite the Jewish community considering it a highly controversial project.

Orthodox and Conservative movements within the Jewish faith believed that in-ground burial was singularly acceptable. Being a reform temple, the most liberal of movements within the Jewish religion, the congregation believed that above-ground interment was an acceptable method of burial citing Genesis 23:19 and Abraham's burial next to his wife Sarah in the above-ground tomb, the Cave of Machpelah, near the city of Hebron in Israel. With the addition of niches for the inurnment of cremated congregants, which many sects of the Jewish religion believed was an abomination, the controversy of the mausoleum being closely associated with a Jewish temple rose to an even more fevered pitch.

As the ceremony ended and the procession made its way from the sanctuary to the mausoleum, Warren and I walked side-by-side at the rear of the crowd. He didn't speak, but I could see his radar-like eyes dart from person-to-person; he looked tense.

"Looking for the killer?" I asked, certain he couldn't tell a thing by ogling the back of people's heads.

"You'd be surprised what I can see from back here. For instance, that couple over there?" Warren discretely pointed at a middle-aged couple. The man wore a dark blue suit; the woman a green dress. "They're married but don't like each other much. See how they're standing? Just close enough to be a couple, but far enough away to make sure they don't touch. If he were any kind of a husband, he would take her hand and console her. Then, there's the guy with his head down." Warren indicated with a nod of his head a heavy set man at the edge of the crowd. "He's covering up something. It's all in the body language."

"Couldn't he just be a sorrowful friend?" I asked.

"He could be," Warren said. "But not in this case."

"How do you know?"

"I'm a detective. I know everything. Haven't you learned that yet?"

I forgot to add the word "cocky" to Warren's description. But in all fairness, in each of the situations I found myself part of in my past adventures, he and Sheriff Berry were accurate in their pronouncements of caution regarding my getting into potentially dangerous situations. And they were Johnny on the spot to bail me out when I did. I guess being on the job for so long gave them the right to have a slanted perspective.

We filed into the Cohen Indoor Mausoleum, an elegant two-story air conditioned marble building that was constructed as the second phase of the project and named after the primary donor. The large colorful hand-crafted stained glass windows at the back of each hall splashed shards of colored light onto the carpeted floor and the polished marble walls that further reflected the scenes in a spectrum of colors. It was a dazzling display of human and divine artistry. Warren and I sat in the back on chairs placed snuggly in the corridor.

"Tell me Detective, why would the Sheriff's Office be so interested in a murder that happened in Boca Raton? I thought the Boca police had jurisdiction here."

"Professional courtesy."

"Because?"

"I'm not at liberty to tell you, Baker. But suffice it to say, I'm working closely with the local authorities."

"The departments are talking to each other then? Glad to hear it. It's only taken sixty years."

"What do you mean by that?"

"You've never read about the Lazzari case? Happened in 1948. A double homicide. Could have been solved if the Palm Beach Sheriff's Office and the Boca Police had bothered talking to each other. Unfortunately, they didn't. The case remains unsolved to this very day."

"Well, I don't know what happened way back then, but today we're trying to solve this one." Warren reached into his pocket, pulled out his cell phone and proceeded to thumb through it. When he found what he was looking for, he stuck the phone in front of me. "Thought you might like to see this," he whispered.

I sucked air as I looked at his phone. It was Mort. Dead as a door nail. His crumpled body dressed in khaki pants and green pullover shirt lay beside a fountain and next to a black marble bench in the outdoor rotunda of the mausoleum. His head lay in a pool of blood with his open blank eyes staring into space. His pudgy face seemed to ask the question "why?" An empty bronze vase, I took for the murder weapon, lay on its side next to him. Pink rose petals along with a dozen long stems with a few remnant petals were strewn about his body in a nondescript pattern. I wondered if they were byproducts of the blow to Mort's head or part of some sick sign left by the murderer.

I opened my mouth to respond but Warren brought his index finger to his lips and shushed me as the ceremony was about to begin. I simply nodded my acknowledgement and sat there in shocked silence at what I had just seen.

The brief ceremony was interspersed with prayers after which Mort's casket was placed into the crypt. Afterward, we were invited to join the family back at the temple to share condolences with the bereaved. It was here I figured I would learn the answers to my questions.

Warren and I walked back to the temple in silence. Once inside, the detective made a bee line for the refreshment table, piled his plate with finger sandwiches then took up post in the back of the hall where he could scrutinize the entire crowd. I was more discrete. I selected vegetables and dip in an effort to keep my middle-aged waistline from expanding; besides, I wanted to save room for tonight's restaurant de jour.

Ever since I semi-retired, Rosa and I decided to eat out more and cook in less. Since she had more time to plan these outings, she always selected the evening's restaurant and acted as chauffeur. I never knew where we were going until we arrived. Tonight I hoped for steak, perhaps Outback?

"You look familiar. Were you a friend of Mort's?"

I looked down to see a sprig of an elderly woman standing next to me. She was dressed in an attractive grey suit, weighed all of one hundred pounds and stood about five feet tall, just under a foot shorter than I was.

"I knew him," I said. "I wrote an article about him several years ago." At my explanation, her eyes lit up.

"Yes, of course. You're that reporter from Sunshine Media. I recognize you from your photo next to the article."

"Yes, ma'am. Shea Baker." I extended my hand. Her frail thin fingers wrapped around it warmly.

"Helen Lechner." Her grey eyes twinkled and her smile revealed teeth that could have used a set of Invisalines. "Mort and I served on the mausoleum committee together."

"Say, since you served on the mausoleum committee and are familiar with Jewish funeral customs, do you mind if I ask you a few questions?"

"Not at all, Mr. Baker. What would you like to know?"

"I didn't see any flowers and Mort's casket was closed. The funerals I've attended had an abundance of flowers and mourners were encouraged to view the deceased."

"Well, Mr. Baker, the Jewish religion believes funerals should be simple. No fanfare. Humility is key, so we don't display flowers. But we do offer food to the family after the service or for Shiva. Regarding the casket, if the family wants to view the deceased, that's okay, but it's usually done in a separate room, before the funeral. Anything else you'd like to know?" She smiled sweetly.

"Not at the moment, but if I think of something, I'll be sure to ask." We stood there in silence for a few seconds.

"Ironic don't you think that Mort should die and be buried in the same building he spent seven years of his life helping to construct?"

"Yes, ma'am. I'd say it is."

"If you knew the whole story, you'd think it more than ironic," she said.

My brows shot up. "What do you mean?"

Helen looked up at me; her smile faded into a frown. She scanned the room furtively, extended a bony index finger in my direction, and beckoned me closer. I bent down. She brought her fingers to her nose and pinched her nostrils.

"Something stinks around here. Someone needs to investigate." Her nasally whisper was barely audible.

"Why is that?" I whispered back, my journalistic instincts kicking in.

"Too many people dying, including Mort."

"Have there been others?"

"Not in the same manner as Mort, but dead just the same. And they didn't have one foot in the grave, if you get my drift."

"I do," I assured her. "But, if these folks weren't on their last legs and you know something, you should tell the police."

"Can't," she said, her grey eyes brimming with tears. "I could be next."

"Ah, Mr. Baker. So good of you to come to Mort's funeral."

I looked up to see Rabbi Joseph Larkin. He extended his hand; we shook.

"Wouldn't have missed it," I said with a smile.

I turned back to Helen. I really wanted to speak with her more, but she had vanished into the sea of mourners.

"You gave the temple a considerable boost when your article first came out about the mausoleum," Larkin said. "We sold several crypts because of it."

"A small percentage is all I ask," I said with a smile.

"I'm afraid the statute of limitations on commissions ran out long ago." Larkin let out a soft laugh.

"I thought you had retired several years ago and that Rabbi Wasserman was now senior Rabbi."

"He is, but Mort and I were very close and we went through a lot together building the mausoleum. When his widow asked me to do his service, I just couldn't say 'no.'"

"What do you make of Mort's murder?" I asked in a low voice.

"A horrible event," Larkin said, shaking his head. "And to be killed right in the mausoleum."

"Do they have any leads?"

"Not that I've heard." Rabbi Larkin greeted and shook hands with several mourners.

"You know, he contacted me just before his murder."

"Really? What did he want?"

"He wanted to meet me at the mausoleum." Though I felt the rabbi an honest person, I held back part of the message—that Mort had something so important to say he wanted me to record and that he asked me to bring my camera. Maybe I was being as cautious as Warren.

"Is that *all* the message said?"

"No. He sent me a Bible verse about the Israelites crossing the Jordan River and taking stones from it. Then he referenced a magazine article . . . something about there not being any historically documented proof that the Israelites had, in fact, made their forty-year trek as the Bible states."

"Ah, yes. I'm aware of the article," Larkin said, nodding his head. "Mort and I discussed it at considerable length."

"Of what great significance are these stones?"

"If they exist, they are holy artifacts and go all the way back to the Exodus, when the Israelites crossed into the Promised Land."

"Go on." I stepped closer to make sure I heard every word of his explanation.

"Well, it's like this—" But before Rabbi Larkin could continue, an elderly man interrupted us.

"Fine service, Rabbi." The man shook Larkin's hand. "Mort was a good man. We'll certainly miss him, especially at our weekly poker game. Right Rabbi?" The man let out a robust laugh, gave Larkin a wink, and moved on toward the refreshments.

A flush of pink crept up Larkin's face and he looked at me as though the cat had just leapt from the bag.

"Joe Greene." Larkin nodded toward the man's back as he walked away. "A member of our visiting committee."

"And, apparently, your poker group."

"That too."

Just as Larkin was about to continue his explanation of the Exodus, a middle-aged couple approached.

"Perhaps if you could come by my home next week we could sit down and talk without being interrupted," he whispered.

"I'll do that," I said.

I left Larkin and threaded my way through the mourners. While I spoke to a number of people, what I really wanted to do was to chat with Helen again. After a considerable search, however, she was nowhere to be found. At least I had caught her name. I would give her a call next week and see if she had anything more to say.

"Seen and heard enough?" Warren's unexpected voice made me jump and sent a crick into my neck.

"Don't sneak up of me like that." My furrowed brow and well-defined scowl accentuated my genuine annoyance.

"Sorry, Baker, didn't know you were so sensitive."

"Well . . . did you find the killer? Did he, in fact, return to the scene of the crime?" I massaged my neck to disperse the knot.

"Perhaps. And I noted a couple of possibilities, including that sweet little old lady who you seemed to take a lot of interest in."

I pulled back. "You've got to be kidding."

"Nope. In a case like this, everyone's a potential suspect." Warren clasped his hands behind him, rocked back in forth on his heels, and perused the room,

"Including me?"

He stopped rocking and locked his eyes onto mine. His stare could burn a hole into your very skull. "Especially you, Baker. Don't forget, our familiarity with your modus operandi from your last two escapades suggests you know much more than you let on. It may take time, but we'll find out what that is, unless, of course, you decide to volunteer the information."

"Detective," I said, holding up my hands in surrender, "I told you, I came to pay my respects to Mort's wife and family."

"Baker, I'd believe you if, in fact, you had spent even one second seeking out the bereaved family. But you haven't, so that excuse is as malodorous as dog poop. Want to tell me what's really going on? Is this another one of your biblical mysteries?" His tone was as stern as his facial expression.

I took a deep breath. In all actuality, he was right on the money—Mort's death did look like it was turning into another mystery based on scripture with the exception of one thing . . . I really didn't know anything. All I had was a message from a dead guy about some ancient stones from the Bible, and a little old lady who thinks people at the temple are dying all too frequently. These two pieces of information didn't add up to squat.

I opened my mouth to speak, but just about that time Warren's cell phone vibrated. He pulled it from his pocket and placed it to his ear.

"Roger. I'm leaving now," he said in a soft tone. He returned the phone to his pocket. "This isn't over Baker. You know it, and I know it. I just hope whatever you've gotten yourself into won't leave Rosa a widow. I'm sure she's had just about enough of your shenanigans." Without further conversation, he made his way from the room.

With Warren gone, I perched my hat on my head and doubled back to the mausoleum to see where Mort had been killed. It wasn't as if I had a morbid curiosity about these things, but I did want to see the place where it happened, look around a little, and see if I could make sense of it. What was it about the mausoleum that was so compelling Mort wanted me to bring my recorder and camera?

Since all the mourners were still in the temple extending condolences to the family, all was quiet at the mausoleum. Opposite the Cohen Indoor Mausoleum in which Mort was interred, I walked through a lovely and lush garden, bordered by tall palm trees and a high ficus hedge. It was a serene spot dotted with blooming hibiscus and a blue sky vine. A brick pathway meandered by a small brook dotted with benches—quite the spot to remember a loved one or meditate about the meaning of life . . . and death.

The path led from the gardens to a breezeway called the Rosenblum Chapel, named after a couple that donated a substantial sum to the mausoleum building fund for the privilege of having the structure named for them. I remembered from my long ago magazine article that the mausoleum had been built in two phases. The Rosenblum Chapel, with its adjoining Jaffe Rotunda, and Horowitz Hall, were open air structures built in the first phase of construction. A long wide corridor of inlaid brick in a herringbone design ran down the length of the interior of the Rosenblum Chapel. Embedded in the center in black brick was the Star of David. Along its three walls were rows of crypts and niches. I took out my cell phone and snapped several photos.

At the far end of the chapel, a doorway to the left led to the Jaffe Rotunda. Here, a curved wall of crypts surrounded the centerpiece of the room, a circular fountain. It was next to the fountain and black marble bench with the inscription "Soul Mates Forever" that Mort had bought the farm—a bash to the head with a heavy bronze vase that left pink rose petals strewn about the body. Though the place had been cleaned up, I could still see muted brown stains on the brick floor where his blood had pooled beside the bench. I supposed with time and an abundance of Florida sunshine it would fade. I took photos of the crime scene from a myriad of angles.

Opposite the Rosenblum Chapel and adjacent to the Jaffe Rotunda, a large entrance led to the Horowitz Hall that accommodated more crypts. Several private areas, enclosed by wrought iron fencing and gates, allowed loved ones to be interred together, a kind of family plot. At the end of the hall, one entered the garden once again. I shot a couple of photos of this corridor as well. As I did, I noticed a man dressed in a long black coat enter the viewfinder. He took one look at me and abruptly did an about face, walking briskly away. I thought this odd so I proceeded after him, but by the time I reached the exterior of the garden, the man was gone.

I quickly reviewed the photos I had taken. Though I never caught the man's full face, I did catch the back of him as he made his exit. He looked very much like the man Warren had pointed out at the service that he thought was hiding something. And, in fact, he seemed roughly familiar. I couldn't put my finger on it right then, but I knew it would come to me. These things always did. Usually as an "eureka moment" while taking a shower or in the middle of the night.

Finished with my photos and tour of the mausoleum, I decided that since I was already in Boca Raton I'd run up to Florida Atlantic University and visit Stella, my part-time research assistant. Her steady part time job between attending classes was at the university library. I met her several years ago when she worked in the library at the north campus of Broward Community College. She helped locate information for my first mystery and proved to be an outstanding researcher. I hired her to do some research for my second mystery as well, and I came to discover she was also a computer geek of the highest order. Finding her hunkered down at the reference desk eyes glued to her monitor was not unusual.

"Hi, little lady," I said in my best John Wayne imitation. I bowed slightly as I took off my hat. She looked up at me with a wide smile that revealed gapped front teeth and twinkling blue eyes.

"Boss. So good to see you." In an instant, her smile was gone. Her brow crinkled and her baby blues took on a puzzled look. She pointed to the top of her head, then to the top of mine.

"What?" I asked, spreading my hands. Again she pointed to my head. It was then I realized I was still wearing the kippah from the temple. I quickly pulled it from my head and made a mental note to wash and return it the next time I was over that way.

"Thanks," I said with a smile. "Finding anything of world-altering proportions?"

"Not since our last exciting mystery." A wink of her right eye punctuated her distinct British accent. "How's the new book coming?"

"Right along, though I've had to take a little detour. Thought you might like an assignment."

"You know me. I'm always up for one of your adventures. Another mystery?" Her brows arched expectantly.

"Perhaps. Can we go someplace more . . . private?"

"I get a break in ten. Why don't you go up to the third floor and look at Author Jaffe's unusual book collection? You'll enjoy it. Besides, it's quiet there and we can talk." Stella handed me a colorful brochure entitled The Jaffe Center for Book Arts.

I made my way to the collection not knowing what to expect. Growing up, I had an estranged relationship with books and libraries, like two magnets—both with north poles. But I did write a lot and had an innate ability to string words together in a cohesive way. Yet, my biggest asset was being a good listener and asking the right questions.

Instead of going to college, I joined the Air Force. Once they realized my insatiable curiosity, which drove my commanding officer nuts, coupled with my literary talents they assigned me to the public relations department where I wrote a variety of articles for the base newspaper. I interviewed top brass, visiting celebrities, servicemen from unusual backgrounds, and even did some hard core reporting on new aircraft and equipment. It was this military assignment—on the job training by the seat of my pants—that I learned formal journalism. People liked what I wrote and many of my articles wound up in the Stars and Stripes, an international paper designed for and read by those in the armed services.

After a career in the service, I retired to Deerfield Beach on Florida's southeast coast with Rosa. Having too much time on my hands and convinced that the turf at local golf courses would remain much more pristine without Shea Baker hacking into it, I went back into journalism part time writing for Sunshine Media. I get my picture in a small . . . very small . . . photo at the end of each article. Even after my first Bible based mystery *Holy Land* became a best seller, I continued to write for the publication. I wanted to keep my hand in the trade.

The Jaffe Center for Book Arts turned out to be a museum of sorts. In it, books of every imaginable size—tiny to huge; shape—round, square, cubed, even shaped like a purse; type—musings, politics, geography; medium—paper, wood, metal, fabric; and color—every hue of the rainbow were displayed in glass cases and on shelves. The Center's mission was to celebrate books as art. Believe me the emphasis was on "art." It truly was a dazzling display of the most unusual books I'd ever seen. After seeing them, it gave me a new perspective and made me wonder: What is a book?

About the time I was examining an extraordinary object constructed of hand-made paper and carved pop-up pages, Stella approached me iPad in hand. Her outfit—black pants and V-necked print blouse—was quite tame from her typical flamboyant attire.

"What happened to the pink and black stripped tights, short pink skirt, and hair done up in pink bows?" I asked. She had worn such an outfit to one of our former meetings at a coffee shop. All eyes were on her extravagant pink and black color palette.

"Boss, I can't wear that every day. Today's my conservative day."

"Perfectly understandable," I said, nodding my head. I wondered if I should come by tomorrow just to see what was on for the fashion show.

"By the way, what's up with that?" She pointed to my felt fedora.

"It keeps my head warm."

"Boss," Stella said, hands on hips, "this is Florida. It's hot here."

"Yeah, well, it adds character. What do you think?" I set the dark green hat on my head, pulled the brim down on one side and struck a pose in my best rendition of a GQ model.

"I have to admit it does add character." Stella punctuated her sentence with a wink.

"Enough of that," I said, removing the hat. "Back to business. I'm not sure where we'll go with this, but I need you to look into something for me."

"Shoot," she said. For emphasis, she pulled up the short sleeve of her blouse to reveal a colorful tattoo of John Wayne riding a stallion with reins in his mouth and brandishing six-guns in both hands. I had seen the image before, when I first met Stella. She told me she was a devoted fan of The Duke, something we had in common, and knew the script from every one of his films by heart. She had then recited dialogue from his 1969 popular movie "True Grit" with a British accent. I followed with a portrayal of The Duke's famous swagger. We both fell out laughing; neither one of us was very good.

"I need you to find out the names, occupation, cause of death, and obituaries . . . anything you can get on anyone who has been buried for the past two years in the mausoleum on city property built by Boca Raton's Temple Beth Shalom. I also want you to find out everything you can on a Helen Lechner."

"Stella typed away on her tablet then looked at me with raised brow. "That doesn't sound like a biblical mystery to me."

"Maybe not, but it's related to one." I gave her a copy of Mort Saul's email. After she read it, I told her about my conversation with Helen.

"But how are these deaths related to your friend and the Exodus?"

"That's what we're going to find out."

"Gotcha Boss."

"Now, what university professor can you direct me to who is an expert in Jewish history?"

"That's easy. We've only got two. But do you want the conservative or liberal one?"

My eyebrows shot up.

"They're at opposite ends of the spectrum on their faith and history," Stella said.

I shrugged my shoulders. "I guess I should speak with both."

She gave me the name of the two professors—Meyer Belinsky and Bob Clark.

Rosa must have read my mind because tonight's restaurant du jour turned out to be Outback Steak House. We sat in a booth in the corner and ordered a blooming onion along with drinks—wine for her, beer for me. That would get us started.

"How was the funeral?" Rosa took a sip of her Merlot.

"Fine. If funerals can be fine." I dipped my onion into the special sauce provided and savored the crispy fried outer crust and sweet meat of the onion. I washed it down with a swig of beer. "Saw your buddy there."

"My buddy?" She looked at me quizzically.

"Detective Warren."

"Oh, you mean Stan. How *is* he?"

Rosa's tone of endearment sent a shade of green surging through my emotional channels. But it wasn't her fault, it was mine. The two had become fast friends ever since she phoned the detective regarding my disappearance and supposed kidnapping at Carrabba's restaurant and again on the occasion of my fling into the python-filled canal up at Lake Okeechobee in my last adventure. It was because of those little escapades, and former ones, that she now had him on speed dial. I guess she was expecting a repeat performance somewhere down the line.

"He's okay," I said. "Taught me the finer points of body language."

"I didn't know you needed a lesson." Rosa's wink and sly grin made it clear she liked whatever body language I had.

"Actually, he's trying to find Mort's killer. Thought by checking out the mourners he might hit pay dirt."

"And did he?"

"Said he had some leads."

"Well, I'm sure Stan will find the person that killed your friend. He's a good detective and it would be awful—" Rosa stopped abruptly as though a light bulb came on. She put down her wine glass, leaned in, and stared hard at me, her eyes narrowing. "Shea, this isn't going to be another one of your mysteries is it? You're not getting involved are you?"

My silence and sheepish expression were all Rosa needed to deduce the answer. She sat back, crossed her arms across her ample bosom and lit into a heated rebuke in Spanish, the translation of which I could only image. Rosa reverted to her native tongue only when she was angry. This was one of those times. Let me just say that even with her one-sided scolding, our table conversation didn't add one decibel to the din of noise already in the restaurant.

Chapter 6

The next morning I tried to cozy up to Rosa but she was still in a huff over last night's silent confession, so I figured I'd hit the office and make a few phone calls. I hoped she would be in a more receptive mood by the afternoon.

My first call was to the university. I was fortunate to find both Meyer Belinsky and Bob Clark in and available for back-to-back appointments in the early afternoon. My next task was to read the scripture Mort referred to so I could ask some educated questions of both men. The person next on my list of phone calls was Dan E. Powell. As evangelist and pastor of one of South Florida's megachurches, Imperial Point Christian Church in north

Fort Lauderdale, Powell had been instrumental in explaining scripture to me during my last two adventures. With an impressive resume and theological connections around the world, I wanted to get his take on the Old Testament scripture in question before I spoke with either of the professors. Unfortunately, he wasn't in, but his assistant Virginia Boone said she'd give him the message.

Before I departed for the university, I looked up both Belinsky and Clark on the Internet to get a little background on each and supplement the short introduction Stella had given me. Sure enough, Belinsky was a rogue in the Jewish faith and stood out like a man uncircumcised. With his reputation of skepticism of Jewish biblical history, until, of course, it was proven by tangible evidence, and the many books he'd written on the subject, I wondered just why he was in the history department at all. On the opposite end of the spectrum was Clark. He believed in the literal translation of Jewish scripture, and that even to this day, it remained historically accurate. He had written just about as many articles and books taking an opposing view as Belinsky. How these two professors with profoundly differing views wound up at the same university and in the same department was a mystery. But then I had to remember, universities thrived on controversy, as long as it was done in the name of free speech and didn't affect funding, especially from deep-pocketed alumni.

The campus of Florida Atlantic University was a sprawling collection of buildings on the north side of Glades Road just east of I95. I made my way to the Arts and Letters building, took the elevator up to the fourth floor, and was greeted by Penelope Hampton, the receptionist. I handed her my business card.

"Professor Belinsky is expecting you. His office is the third one on the left." Penelope pointed to a string of doors down a long hallway. His door was open.

Belinsky was behind his desk, feet propped on top, eyes closed. He was stroking his dark beard with one hand and tapping a pencil against his head with the other.

"Am I interrupting anything?"

The professor came to an immediate upright position and rose behind his desk.

"Sorry, I was deep in thought. Trying to plan my trip to Israel for an archeological dig. You must be Shea Baker." He walked toward me and stuck out his hand. "Meyer Belinsky. I've read several of your articles."

I extended my hand not knowing whether that was a compliment or not. "I appreciate you seeing me on such short notice."

"I just happen not to have any classes this afternoon. You caught me at a good time. Please have a seat." Belinski pointed to two chairs opposite his desk, both heaped with books and papers. "Oh, excuse me," he said. He quickly removed the items and found another place for them—on the floor. "What can I do for you?" he continued, once settled in his chair.

"I wondered if you could give me your perspective on the Exodus? I understand that you have a take on the event that contradicts the Bible."

Belinsky looked at his watch and chuckled. "How much time have you got?"

"CliffNotes will suffice," I said, not wanting to take up that much of the professor's time.

"Very well then, here is the CliffNotes version." The professor sat back in his chair and crossed his arms. "The event never happened."

Deafening silence hung in the air as I waited for further explanation. None came.

"That's it?" I finally asked.

"That's it if you want the CliffNotes version. If you want a more detailed explanation, it will take a few more minutes."

"Will thirty be enough?"

"It's a start," Belinsky said.

"Do you mind if I tape your explanation? I'd like to make sure I hear and understand correctly what you're saying. It's the old reporter in me." I pulled out my digital recorder and turned it on. The professor settled back in his chair.

"An archaeologist uses the Bible as a reference for both the location and time of a specific biblical event and then creates a testable hypothesis. He proves or disproves this premise through fieldwork, that's 'archeological digs' for the layman. Ancient texts are used to supplement archaeological sources and make sense of the leftover traces and artifacts of ancient cultures. Are you with me so far?"

I nodded. His explanation took me back to what I'd learned in my high school classes: "a *hypothesis* refers to a provisional idea whose merit requires research and evaluation."

"Good. Now we'll get to the subject you want me to tell you about—the Exodus. The Bible explains that the Exodus happened at the time of Ramesses II, known as Ramesses the Great. He was the third pharaoh of the Nineteenth Dynasty of Egypt, born in 1303 CE and died in 1213 CE. At the time of Ramesses' reign, the border between Canaan and Egypt was carefully controlled. The main road that stretched from the delta along the coast of northern Sinai to Gaza and into the heart of Cannan was of the utmost importance to the pharaonic regime. Along this route, Pharaoh established a sophisticated system of forts, granaries, and wells. Each was established at a day's marching distance along the entire length of this road, which was called the Ways of Horus. The wells, forts, and granaries were built to accommodate the imperial army when it crossed the Sinai Peninsula. How do we know this? A relief engraved on a wall in the temple of Amun at Karnak depicts the road, and the remains of these forts were uncovered in the 1970s by Eliezer Oren of Ben-Gurion University.

"Papyrus records from this time indicate commanders of the numerous forts in the kingdom monitored the movements of foreigners very closely. If a great mass of people, the Israelites in this case, passed through borders controlled by the pharaonic regime, records would exist. Yet none of the abundant Egyptian sources describing this time refer to the Israelites fleeing Egypt. Not one.

"Besides, any large group of slaves fleeing Egypt would have easily been tracked down through the heavily guarded route, first by the Egyptian Army chasing it from the delta, and then by the soldiers who guarded the forts in northern Sinai and Cannan.

"The Merneptah Stele, a black granite slab containing hieroglyphics written by the Ancient Egyptian king Merneptah, refers to the Israelites as a group of people already living in Cannan at this time, but we have not one single word about early Israelites in Egypt. There are no monumental inscriptions on walls of temples, in tombs, or on papyri. As a matter of fact, Israel is completely absent in reference as a friend, foe, or enslaved nation."

I thought of the Bible's rendition—Israelites crossing the Red Sea with the Egyptian army hot on its heels, God parting the waters so the Israelites could cross on dry land, the drowning of the Egyptians and their horses once the Israelites crossed into safety.

"Divine intervention as the Bible suggests?" I asked.

Belinsky raised a skeptical eyebrow.

"If more than a million Israelites wandered in the Sinai for forty years, wouldn't you think there would be some remnants of their stay there? Except for the Egyptian forts, not a single campsite or sign of occupation exists in Sinai from before the time of Ramesses II to his immediate successors. And it's not for lack of trying to find them." At this, Belinsky rested his elbows on his desk and leaned forward.

"None of the numerous archeological surveys from the regions in the peninsula have yielded any evidence. Not the most miniscule shard of pottery, not a single dwelling, not even the trace of an encampment. Of course, what I've just told you is the shortened version. There's much, much more to the story."

"So it's all fiction? Moses, the liberation of the Israelites, their crossing the desert into the Promised Land? All of it?"

"Evidence of the account of the Exodus on the scale that the Bible asserts and at the time and place today's understanding suggests is nonexistent," the professor said.

"So there's no room for God's hand in any of this?"

"Evidence, Mr. Baker. Evidence is the only thing scientists, archeologists, and historians have to go on."

"If no evidence exists, then the crossing of the Jordan River and the story of the twelve stones are fictitious too?" I asked.

The professor stiffened. "What do you know about the twelve stones?" His tone was more accusatory than curiosity.

"Nothing," I said, taken aback by his abrupt change of tone. "Only what I read in the Bible. I was hoping to find out more from you."

The professor looked at his watch. "I hate to have to cut this short, but it's getting late. I just remembered that I have an appointment and must run." He rose from his chair. This, in no uncertain terms, was my cue to leave.

"Well, thank you for your time, Professor. Perhaps I can get the answer from your colleague Professor Clark. I'm to see him next."

At this suggestion, a rush of pink rose from the professor's neck and flushed onto his face.

"Well, just a minute," he stammered, waving a hand in my direction. "Perhaps I do have a few more minutes." He sat back down; so did I. His eyes became glazed and his stare appeared distant.

"Professor?"

"Oh, sorry, sorry. I was just thinking about something." He leaned across his desk. "I lead an archeological dig every summer in Israel and include my top student. I realize this is kind of short notice, but why don't you come? Not for the whole time, of course, but for a week or so. You could see what we do firsthand and maybe even help us find something of great value. It's not glamorous; it's hard work but very rewarding. I'll bet your readers would be fascinated by a personal account. What do you say?" He looked at me wide-eyed and full of expectation.

The offer was a total surprise, but it intrigued me at the same time. To be in the presence of such a notable professor in Israel on an archeological dig? This was an opportunity of a lifetime.

"I'd have to discuss it with Rosa, my wife."

"Bring her along," he said quite animated. "I'll get my sponsors to cover the cost of your trip for you and your wife—travel, accommodations, food, everything. They'd love to have the press coverage. What do you say?" He leaned back, a broad smile on his lips.

With this abrupt about face, I knew Belinsky was wanting or hiding something. I didn't know which. What I did know, however, was that I doubted I could pass up this compelling opportunity. The trip would take me right into the heart of Mort's mystery.

We shook hands as I left and I was to get back to him in a couple of days regarding the trip. I knew it would be a hard sell to Rosa. I'd already had one kidnapping with a harrowing escape in that part of the world, and to be plunked down in it again would not go over very big. Besides, I was already in the doghouse. I'd have to think long and hard about how to approach *mi amour* on this one. Then a brilliant idea came to me. I wanted to rush home, but first I needed to see Professor Clark.

I knocked on Clark's door, which was at the end of the hallway. He called for me to "come in." When I opened the door, he was behind his desk finishing a phone call. He motioned for me to take a seat while he bid the caller adieu. The chair, like that of an airplane seat, was snug against my derriere. I guess they built them for college-aged kids with much less padding than mine.

I eyed Clark from across his desk and introduced myself. He looked like death warmed over. His eyes were glassy and red rimmed with his nose a pronounced shade of red. A box of tissues sat within arm's reach on his desk.

"How can I help you?" He entwined his long fingers, rested them comfortably across his slender midsection, and forced a smile.

"Are you sure this is a good time to see you? Looks like you could use some hot chicken soup and a soft bed."

"I'm fine, just allergies." He pulled a tissue from the box, blew into it, and tossed it beneath his desk. I assumed there was a trash can there.

"Just finished visiting with Professor Belinsky. He filled me in on the lack of archeological evidence to support the Exodus. I wanted to get your take on the event. I understand you two are on opposite sides of the fence on this."

"Opposite sides? That's certainly a mild way of putting it." Clark's lips stretched across his mouth into two thin lines.

"Do you mind if I tape this? It's only for reference." Clark flicked his hand in a gesture for me to 'go ahead.'

"Do you dispute Professor Belinsky's stand that there is no archeological evidence or ancient text to support the Bible's assertion that the Israelites escaped the Egyptians, spent forty years wandering in the desert, and finally entered Canaan?"

"Yes and no," said Clark. He pulled a tissue from the box and wiped away tears at the corners of his irritated eyes. "If we only look at today's physical evidence, as professor Belinsky suggests, his supposition might seem accurate. At this time, there is no tangible proof that this trek occurred. But that's only in light of today's discoveries. Tomorrow, an archeologist might uncover a building, or part of a clay jug, or even something as innocuous as a pile of rocks that would corroborate this event. Does the lack of evidence today dismiss a hypothesis just because tangible evidence has yet to be discovered? Look at what has occurred just in the 20th and 21st Centuries. Man has gone to the moon, we've split the atom, trillions of pieces of information have been captured on thin slices of silicon, and astronomers have found black holes. At the time, scientists hypothesized that these things were possible, yet there was no proof, only years of calculations, trial, and error, and, most of all, expectation."

"I take it you think something will surface that will debunk Belinsky's supposition?"

"I know it will, Mr. Baker." A smug smile etched its way across Clark's lips and his countenance seemed to perk up.

"How can you be so sure, professor?"

"Hope," Mr. Baker. "Hope and faith. Haven't you ever simply accepted something on faith?"

"You mean like the wind?"

"Or gravity, or the warmth of the sun's rays on your face, or love? None of these things can be seen. We can only feel the effects of them on our body and in our heart."

"Well," I said, adjusting myself in the seat, "back to the reason I came to see you. I want to read you a passage from the Old Testament. This is Joshua 4:4-8:

"4 So Joshua called together the twelve men he had appointed from the Israelites, one from each tribe, 5 and said to them, "Go over before the ark of the LORD your God into the middle of the Jordan. Each of you is to take up a stone on his shoulder, according to the number of the tribes of the Israelites, 6 to serve as a sign among you. In the future, when your children ask you, 'What do these stones mean?' 7 tell them that the flow of the Jordan was cut off before the ark of the covenant of the LORD. When it crossed

the Jordan, the waters of the Jordan were cut off. These stones are to be a memorial to the people of Israel forever.

[8] *So the Israelites did as Joshua commanded them . . . And the stones are there to this day."*

"I'm familiar with this passage. But why are you so interested in these particular verses?"

"A friend suggested I read them. I don't really know why."

Clark leaned toward me, a curious look on his face. "Perhaps your friend would like to come back with you at another time so we could all talk about it together."

I shook my head. "That's not possible."

"Why not?" he asked. All of sudden, Clark inhaled deeply and sneezed into his tissue. He wiped his nose, tossed it under his desk, and pulled another from the box.

"My friend's dead," I said. "Died before he could explain it to me."

Clark sat back and let out a sigh. "I'm sorry to hear that. And you think his death had something to do with these verses?"

"I don't know. I'm just trying to understand the scripture."

Clark looked deep in thought. "What was your friend's name?"

"Mort Saul," I said.

"The man that was murdered in Temple Beth Shalom's mausoleum?" Clark was wide-eyed.

"One and the same. His funeral was yesterday. Did you know him?"

"I knew of him, from the construction of the mausoleum. It was quite a bold and controversial move." Clark dabbed at his red tearing eyes.

"So I've heard."

"So why would Mort Saul send you this specific text from the Bible?"

"Does it mean something to you?" I asked.

"Maybe. Maybe not. Did he reference anything else? Another verse perhaps?"

"Not a verse, but he sent me a link to an article that refuted the Bible's story of the Exodus. It was written by professor Belinsky."

"Curious, very curious," said Clark.

"What do you mean?"

Clark sneezed again. "I'm sorry, Mr. Baker. Maybe you were right after all, and I need to go home."

Darn. We were just getting to the heart of the matter. I left Clark with his allergies and box of tissues, hoping I wouldn't come down with the bird flu or some sort of exotic disease that could be transmitted to someone sitting across his desk.

****

Rosa was making Spanish Bean soup when I got home. I wrapped my arms around her, gave her a kiss on the nape of her neck, and snuggled my lips close to her ear. Now I would pop my brilliant question.

"How would you like a second honeymoon in an exotic country?"

Rosa stopped stirring. "Is this your way of making up?"

"You know I can make up better than that." I kissed her ear. "I just thought you'd be interested in going someplace . . . well . . . a bit out of the ordinary."

"I'm listening," she said.

I turned her around and planted a warm wet one on her lips.

"How would you like to visit Israel, tour the Holy Land, maybe slip down to Egypt and see the pyramids? The history professor I saw today, Meyer Belinsky, has invited us on an archeological dig in Israel he's conducting, all expenses paid. I thought it would be a good opportunity for us to get away, sort of a second honeymoon."

Rosa crossed her arms over her chest. "Out of the clear blue sky a professor you don't even know invites you on a trip half way around the world all expenses paid. Does that make any sense?" She eyed me suspiciously. "Does this have anything to do with Mort Saul?"

Once again, I was caught off guard, my silence loud and clear. I braced myself for Rosa's diatribe, but to my utter astonishment, she surprised me.

"Look Shea," she said, cupping my face in her warm hands, "I know I can't stop you when your mind's made up about these things, but the last time you went to Israel I wasn't around, and I almost lost you. This time, I'm not willing to take that risk. Besides, I've always wanted to walk where Jesus walked and see King Tut's Tomb. And an archeological dig sounds like fun. So, if you go, I go, but rest assured," she said, shaking her index finger in my direction, "I'll be keeping a close eye on you." She kissed me on the cheek and turned back to her soup.

I stood there dumbfounded not sure whether this was a positive or negative turn of events.

Chapter 7

I received a call from Virginia Boone the next morning. My appointment with Dr. Powell was set for that afternoon at 3:00 p.m. After what Belinsky had told me about the non-Exodus, I was eager to hear what Powell had to say about the Israelites wandering in the desert, crossing both the Red Sea and the Jordan River, and the twelve stones. In the meantime, I phoned Stella.

"Hi, Boss." Her perky British voice was refreshing.

"Any luck finding out about the folks buried at the mausoleum and Helen Lechner?"

"Second things first," she chuckled. "Here's the scoop on Helen. She's an 87-year-old widow. Her husband, Norman, who owned a seafood distribution company in

New York, died two years ago when his car plunged into a canal on a rainy night. He was buried in the temple mausoleum. They have three children all of whom live in New York. She was a stay-at-home mom. They came to Boca Raton as snow birds, then moved permanently after Norman retired at age 55. She now lives by herself in The Addison North, an upscale Boca Raton condo on A1A. Been a member of the temple for thirty years." Stella took a breath. "I'll email all this to you, Boss, along with her phone number and address. Anything else you need to know about her?"

I wondered if Helen's husband was one of the deceased she had included in the "smelly" situation?

"That's a good start. See what you can find out about the car accident—perhaps a police or news report."

"You think there's something fishy about his death?" Stella let out a chuckle. "Sorry, Boss, I couldn't help it."

I let out a laugh of my own. "Not that I'm aware of, but let's make sure we haven't overlooked anything. Now, what about the others?"

"I'm still working on that. It's taking me a bit longer than I thought to get all the information. How about we meet at Java Joe's tomorrow at 3:00 p.m.? I should have everything by then."

Just as I hung up, I received an email from Belinsky. He reiterated his invitation for Rosa and me to join him and his wife on the archeological dig and restated that the trip would be all expenses paid, in exchange for the magazine coverage. Of course, I needed to clear this with Susan, my editor at Sunshine Media, but felt certain she would be ecstatic about it. My next call was to her.

"Shea, good to hear from you. I was just about to call you. I've got a new assignment for you." Susan, a thirty-something knock-'em-dead blonde, was an accomplished editor that juggled five magazines. We had worked together for years and I was her go-to writer. I loved working with her, and so far, the feeling was mutual.

"What have you got?" I asked. Susan always reserved high profile interviews for me.

"Taylor Swift will be in town for a concert in a few weeks and I want you to interview her. It's all set up."

"I'm not your guy," I said without hesitation. "Maybe you can get one of your younger writers who is into her to take on the project."

"But we cater to readers *your* age. You can supply a perspective we just can't get from a younger writer." In my mind's eye, I could see Susan's coral painted lips pursed in a pout.

"I appreciate your thinking of me, but I have something far more provocative to cover and it will take me out of the country. Was just about to call you to talk about it. I think readers would be most interested, especially those in Palm Beach."

"What is it," Susan asked with reserved enthusiasm.

I relayed to Susan my conversation with Belinsky and his invitation to include me on his archeological dig, all expenses paid.

"What should I tell him?"

"It's not the kind of subject we usually cover, Shea, but since Belinsky is a professor of Jewish history and a well-known figure at FAU, perhaps we could make an exception. You'll need to pull in a strong connection with the FAU students vying for the coveted position to join the professor for the dig. Interview the students, both the one who is selected and others in the class. Get their perspective, then tie it into the experience by following the selected student once you're on site. I think it'll work. Of course, you'll have to do your own photography. We can't afford to send a photographer, so make sure you take a good camera. And take lots of shots. We'll decide which ones to use after you write the article."

"Will do," I said, relieved to have Susan's blessings. "In the meantime, I have a lot of research to do to give context to the story, so I'm going to concentrate on that. The article will be great."

"It better be. I'm putting myself out on a limb here."

After I hung up with Susan, I emailed Belinsky that Rosa and I would be honored to join him and his wife and that the magazine would cover the trip with a feature story in one of their fall editions. To him, this news would be as exciting as finding a long lost relic.

The professor must have been chomping at the bit for my affirmative reply because he emailed me right back. The message included flight and accommodations information along with an itinerary. It looked like a well-organized trip.

****

Powell, a tall man in his mid-seventies with a full head of brown hair lightly seasoned with gray, shook my hand warmly.

"I'm so delighted to see you again. It's been far too long since our last conversation. Please have a seat." He gestured at the two brown leather wing back chairs across from his desk.

His office was as I remembered it—cherry book case with photos, books and greenery tastefully arranged on the shelves, matching desk and credenza, a small round conference table in one corner. It brought back memories of when I had sat around that table with some world-renowned men—an archeologist, theologian, forensic scientist and museum curator—and discussed Holy Land artifacts.

"Thanks for seeing me on such short notice. It's just that I'm—"

"Involved with another biblical mystery," Powell said finishing my sentence.

I cocked my head to one side. "Why would you say that?"

"Virginia has a keen sense for these things and gave me the heads up. She isn't wrong is she?"

I hesitated, unsure whether to confirm or deny the question.

"Let's just say that I'm not quite sure; however, what we discuss today may sway me to one side or the other."

"Fair enough. What would you like to know?"

I relayed my conversations with Belinsky about the Exodus. Powell listened attentively.

"Let me ask you something Shea, are you the kind of guy who can believe something by faith because God said it happened, or do you have to see and touch it to believe?"

I shrugged my shoulders. "I guess the reporter in me says I'm mostly the latter kind of guy."

"Well, Belinsky's right about there not being any tangible proof that the Israelites wondered through the Sinai Peninsula for forty years, but he's wrong that the Exodus never occurred."

"What do you mean?"

"This explanation is going to take some time and will go against the grain of what is currently accepted by the world, but if you'll bear with me, I think you'll understand in the end." Powell stared at me with deep blue penetrating eyes set in an oval, practically wrinkle free face.

"I'm all ears."

"I realize your focus is on the Jordan River crossing, but to fully understand that aspect of the Exodus, we need to go back a few years to the beginning when the Israelites crossed the Red Sea and encamped at Mount Sinai. It's going to be a rather lengthy explanation, but when I'm through, you'll understand why I had to go back so far. Let's move to the conference table where I think we'll be more comfortable."

Powell brought out a map of the Middle East, spread it across his conference table, and placed his leather-bound Bible on top. I removed my recorder from my valise, set it on the map, and turned it on. Powell was familiar with this procedure from my former visits with him and had no objection. We sat in chairs slightly opposite each other. What I learned next was the most mind-blowing explanation I'd ever heard.

"The Bible teaches us that the Israelites were slaves of the Egyptians. Numerous times Moses petitioned Pharaoh for their release, but each time he was denied. Finally, God sent ten plagues upon the Egyptian people to help convince Pharaoh to let the Israelites go. After the last plague, death to the first born in each Egyptian household and their animals, Moses finally received permission from Pharaoh to take the Israelites out of Egypt and into Cannan, the land the Lord had reserved for them. The Bible says there were 600,000 men. Of course, if you add wives and children, that figure rises to more than a million. They also took their livestock—camels, cattle, sheep.

"Scripture tells us that the Israelites crossed the Red Sea, the body of water that separates Egypt from today's Saudi Arabia." Powell pointed to the Red Sea on the map, an elongated body of water below the Sinai Peninsula. "The Straits of Tiran on the tip of the peninsula is the most likely place that God parted the waters so the people could march across on dry land. It's also where we're told that the Egyptian army drowned trying to pursue them."

With each explanation, Powell read the corresponding verse from the Bible.

"After the Israelites crossed into the desert, they camped at the base of a tall mountain. We're talking about one perhaps eight to ten thousand feet high. While there, God called Moses up to the mountain and gave him the Ten Commandments. The mountain was called Mount Sinai. At the end of their desert trek, Moses dies and Aaron takes the Israelites into Canaan by crossing the Jordan River." Again, Powell pointed to the Jordan River, a thin ribbon of blue that stretched from the Sea of Galilee southwest to the Dead Sea and eventually into the Red Sea.

"Okay, so what's so difficult to understand about that?" I asked.

"Well," Powell said, "Are you aware of where today's Mount Sinai is said to be?"

"In the Sinai Peninsula I believe."

"You're right. It's here," he said, pointing to the location on the map. "At the base of the mountain is St. Catherine's Monastery, an Eastern Orthodox monastery said to be built over the spot where God spoke to Moses through the burning bush. The mountain is purported to be the Mount Sinai of the Bible. But do you know how that was determined?"

I shook my head. "I'm clueless."

"By Queen Helena, mother of Constantine the Great, the Roman Emperor who reigned from 306 to 337 AD."

"Wait a minute," I said, stunned by this revelation. "Are you saying that Queen Helena decided on her own that this mountain was Mount Sinai?"

"Not exactly. She had help from her son Constantine."

"So these two made the decision to tell the world where Mount Sinai was located?"

"It was probably done innocently enough, but the fact remains, the mountain was selected with little historic evidence to back it up."

"But, how did this happen?"

"It's a somewhat long story, so I'll give you the abbreviated version. Constantine was prone to dreams and supernatural visions throughout his life. When he was emperor, they became a regular part of his reign. I won't bore you with all the background, but suffice it to say that because of these visions he believed he was another Moses selected by God to transform society into a new world order, with him at the helm.

"In one of Constantine's visions, he saw several 'holy sites' in Palestine and commissioned his mother to go there to discover the locations he had foreseen. Helena identified several of these sites, had them excavated, and then built structures on them. The Church of the Holy Sepulcher, over the site where Jesus was crucified and the tomb where he was said to be buried, is one of those sites. She also identified Jebel Musa, Moses' Mountain, as the site of Mount Sinai, even though there was no firm Jewish tradition to support this as the actual site. In fact, Constantine's selection of the Sinai Peninsula for the site of 'God's Mountain' is said to have occurred around the same time that he decided to build a church over the spot in Jerusalem where Christ is said to have ascended.

"The locations where Helena built structures over the places that she identified as 'holy,' such as Golgotha, where Christ was crucified, his tomb, where he was born and where he ascended to heaven, are now said to date to a much earlier time. But tradition is hard to break. Today tourists view these sites as the supposed locations of these sacred events."

"So you're saying that what we know of today as Mount Sinai, isn't the real mountain on which God spoke to Moses? That another site is the real Mount Sinai?"

"That's what history is suggesting."

Again, I was stunned. I'd never heard this before, and I was pretty sure most Christians and Jews hadn't either. If this was indeed the case, why hadn't this been shouted from the roof tops?

"So, if this Mount Sinai isn't the real one, then professor Belinsky is right and there really isn't any evidence that the Exodus occurred, at least not where most people think it did, in the Sinai Peninsula. And, if it didn't occur there, then just where did it occur? Where's the real Mount Sinai?"

"Ah, now that's the most fascinating part of this whole story," Powell said. "The Bible says that the Israelites fled Egypt, crossed the Red Sea, and encamped at the base of a mountain. If the Israelites had crossed into the Sinai, they would still have been in Egypt. This is because the Sinai was back then, and is to this day, part of Egypt. However, if the Israelites fled Egypt, they would have crossed the Red Sea and entered the land of Midian, then part of Arabia and now known as Saudi Arabia. Incidentally, Midian, in the Arabian Peninsula, is also where Moses fled after murdering the Egyptian. It was there he became a shepherd, eventually married Zipporah, one of Jethro's daughters, and had two children.

"It was in that desert that Moses was called by God to a mountain where he encountered the flaming bush. God spoke from the bush and told Moses he was to lead the Israelites out of Egypt to the land of Caanan. In Exodus, this mountain is said to be in Arabia and is referred to as Horeb, the 'Mountain of God.' When Moses leads the Israelites out of Egypt, the Bible again refers to Moses leading them to the Mountain of God. If these two mountains are one and the same, then it's logical to conclude that the mountain of the Exodus is the same mountain where Moses earlier encountered the burning bush. According to Josephus, the first century historian, Mt. Sinai is the highest mountain in the region of the city of Madian in Saudi Arabia. That mountain is Jabal al Lawz, Mountain of Fire."

"Have you ever been there?"

"To Jabal al Lawz? In Saudi Arabia?" Powell let out a friendly laugh. "No, my friend, I haven't been there. It isn't a place you can simply show your passport and waltz into. It takes connections, and the right ones at that. I don't think the Saudis are eager to allow a Christian pastor into their country to tour this sight or archeologists, Jewish or otherwise, to excavate it."

"So where does that leave us? How does this tie into the Jordan River crossing?" I asked.

"I was getting to that. If the Israelites wondered in the Sinai Peninsula, all they had to do is walk northeast and they would have entered Canaan. They wouldn't have had to cross the Red Sea or the Jordan River. However, if they encamped at Jabal al Lawz, they definitely would have had to cross the Red Sea to get into Midian, now Saudia Arabia, and then the Jordan River to reach Canaan." Powell traced this route on the map with his finger. "But, so far, there is no evidence of that."

"So, what I think you're saying is that although today there may not be any evidence of the Exodus, it's not because it didn't happen."

"Yes, that's where faith comes in. Either live by faith or by evidence. It's your choice."

"And if we wait long enough, evidence will back up faith?"

Powell raised his eyebrows. "Isn't that what's been happening throughout history, later generations finding evidence of former civilizations and events?"

"So when the scriptures state that stones in the Jordan River were picked up by one person from each of the twelve tribes of Israel and placed as a memorial on the other side of the river to commemorate the crossing, the Exodus really did happen. We just haven't found evidence of it yet."

"That would be my conclusion," Powell said.

My head was swimming by the time we finished our conversation. I was sure there was much more to this Exodus story, but didn't know what. Maybe I could find out by talking to some historians once I got to Israel. But, I was still puzzled. What did all this fascinating information have to do with Mort's death?

Chapter 8

Our trip to the Middle East was in three short weeks. I had a lot of research to do before then, and I wanted to hear from Stella regarding the death of the temple members. I was sure there was something going on there as Helen seemed sincere and genuinely concerned. I just didn't know what it all meant, and what it had to do with Mort's murder.

I had phoned Stella yesterday and asked if we could put off our meeting until this morning. She had no problem with that, and we met at our usual rendezvous spot at Java Joes in the Barnes and Noble bookstore on Glades Road just across from the FAU campus.

Stella hadn't been kidding that her previous attire had been worn on her conservative day, and it was equally obvious that it was now imprisoned in her closet. Today's outfit consisted of a blouse overlaid with a quilted vest, skirt and brown knee-high boots. It wasn't so much the style of the clothes that made her stand out in a crowd as it was the combination of colors and prints as though someone closed their eyes and simply grabbed something from the closet.

"It's all the rage," she said, noticing my wide eyes and gapping mouth.

"Well," I stammered, "I doubt anyone would ask me to judge a fashion show. I know nothing about it, except—"

"Except what?" Her blue eyes explored my face.

"Except that the outfit just doesn't seem to match. The olive greens and red plaids of the vest don't seem to go with the purple geometrics of the blouse and the blue and white print skirt."

"That's the whole point. Who wants to look like everyone else? Stand out. That's my motto. You know, like Lady Gaga." She placed her hands on her hips and tossed her head back.

I knew who Lady Gaga was—great voice, pretty face. But she obviously had some inner demons to exorcise, thus the reason for her outlandish costumes. So far, I hadn't seen any of those demons in Stella. She seemed well adjusted, had a positive attitude and was quite intelligent. I felt this quirky side—her wardrobe—could all be chalked up to her going through her "university phase." You know, that time when college kids seek to "find themselves" as they push whatever envelope is out there trying to melt into adulthood.

"Look, it doesn't matter to me what you wear," I finally said.

"Glad that's settled," said Stella with a smile.

I bought us both coffee and a cranberry muffin before we settled into a booth for two in the back. Stella plopped her large tote bag onto the bench beside her and began dragging papers from it. She organized them on the table top.

"Here's the scoop, Boss. It seems that of the 135 inurnments and interments at the temple's mausoleum over the past three years, eighty were temple members. The rest were friends or relatives of the member or others who wanted to be buried in a Jewish mausoleum. Causes of death ranged from car accidents, to heart attacks, from strokes to home accidents and murder, as in the case of Mort Saul. Ages ranged from as young as thirty-five to the ripe old age of one-hundred-two, with the majority of deaths occurring in those over seventy-five." She handed me a conveniently organized Excel spreadsheet along with a backup packet of the information.

"I'm really only interested in those buried in the temple mausoleum and whether there is any relationship between them."

Between sips of coffee and nibbling at her muffin, Stella continued.

"Didn't find anything unusual regarding their causes of death, seems all those were legitimate. At least, nothing unusual is listed on the death certificates. Most of the elderly, those over seventy, died from 'natural causes.' The thirty-five-year-old died while riding his bicycle along A1A. He was hit by an elderly driver, Erwin Schloss, but the driver wasn't cited due to the unusually thick early morning fog. He claimed he didn't see the rider. The rest of the deaths are listed there by cause." Stella pointed to the column titled "Cause of Death."

"What about the dates of their deaths? Anything unusual there?" I was looking for something, but I didn't know what.

"Let's see." She looked over her copy of the statistics. "Well, I can tell you that the number of burials seems to have increased each year. For instance, there were 60 funerals last year, around 45 the year prior to that, and 27 the year before that. So far this year, there have been 42. If they keep this up, they could inter as many as one hundred people this year. I guess their marketing program is really working."

"Well, that isn't so unusual. It takes time to market a product and get information out to the consumer. I'm sure it's even more difficult to market a mausoleum. No one really wants to plan ahead, especially for death."

"Yeah. I don't understand it. Shouldn't temple members be dying to get into the mausoleum?" Stella winked at me. "Pun intended."

I laughed. "There's got to be something we're missing here. Maybe a visit to Helen Lechner is in order."

"That's a good idea, Boss. She'll probably be able to tell you something more. I mean, she really didn't tell you much on your first meeting except she thought something wasn't on the up and up. Maybe another meeting will be more productive and she'll give you something to work with."

Stella and I bid each other adieu and I went home to further study the stack of papers she gave me and call Helen.

As I walked to my car, my eyes buried in Stella's statistics, out of the corner of my eye I caught a man beside me with a familiar gait.

"We meet again," he said, keeping pace.

"Yea, the last time we saw each other was at Deerfield Island. It was at the end of the Spear of Destiny mystery, and you had just leveled the proverbial bomb. So what is The Consigned up to this time?" I continued walking hoping the unwelcomed intruder would disappear.

Omar, as I had learned over the course of my involvement in the previous mysteries, was a member of The Consigned, a world-wide clandestine organization that became involved in select events in order to prevent the world from spinning out of control. The group was made up of experts in myriad fields—medicine, archeology, forensics, biology, technology, nuclear medicine, hydrology, physics, etc.—who, at a moment's notice, would intervene in circumstances anywhere on the globe. The group was a-political, a-theological, and "a-" everything. Their only mission was to prevent world chaos. While a noble cause, it was their methods I objected to, like using people without their knowledge or consent . . . me specifically.

"We heard about your new quest. Want to offer our assistance."

I stopped abruptly. "Your assistance?"

"Yes. As a courtesy."

"In the past, you've orchestrated my circumstances to the point of putting my life in serious jeopardy, and now you say you want to offer me your assistance? No thanks. On second thought, just why do you think I need it?" His eyes were dark opaque pools. I tried to see to the bottom of them for the truth.

"Well, this particular mission that you're on, finding Mort's killer, isn't world-altering, like your previous ones."

"Geez," I said, removing my hat and running my fingers through what was left of my thinning hair, "How did you know about Mort? Are you hacking into my email now?" I knew The Consigned had long jelly fish-like tentacles, but didn't think my emails would be that interesting to them.

"I've told you before, Shea, we know everything. I thought you'd have learned that by now." Omar's slicked back dark hair and dark eyes were accentuated by a sly grin.

I'd heard that phrase before from Detective Warren and figured that if he and Omar knew everything, they certainly didn't need me.

"If you know so much, then you could save me a lot of time and energy. Who killed Mort and why?"

"He's not our priority."

"Then what is?"

"The mystery he's involved in; the twelve stones."

It was as though Omar had punched me in the solar plexus. It took me a moment to catch my breath.

"How did you know about that? And what interest does The Consigned have in them?"

"Some things can't be revealed just now, but suffice it to say that The Consigned does have a very intense interest, and we'll be glad to offer you our aid."

"Why can't you people just leave me alone?"

"Can't do," he said unapologetically.

"Why not?"

"Because you're part of us now."

I drew back, my face crinkled in the absurdity. "I'm not part of you."

"You are, whether you like it or not. For some reason, you seem to become involved with potentially world-altering events, or else the world-altering events become involved with you. Either way, you're deeply entrenched. We simply can't let you proceed without our involvement. Expect us at any time." Omar smiled, gave me his trademark two-finger salute, turned, and walked away leaving me dumbstruck.

"I suppose if I *should* need you, I can reach you the usual way?" I called after him. The usual way was to call a toll free number that connected me to 'All Things Middle-Eastern,' an import/export business. I'd ask for Omar Shama, and the receptionist would tell me I have the wrong number. Omar would call me back within minutes.

Omar didn't turn around as he left. He simply raised his hand in the air and waved.

Chapter 9

I had phoned Rabbi Larkin and made an appointment to see him at his home in Boca. With what Powell had told me about Jabal al Lawz perhaps being the real Mt. Sinai, I was interested to get Larkin's take on it and hoped he could shed some light on the twelve stones and their significance as well. I suspected that the ravages of time had taken its toll on their whereabouts, but perhaps some Jewish lore still existed that could pierce the vastness of time and this mystery.

I arrived at the appointed hour to a two story condo in north Boca on the Intracoastal and was greeted by Mark, a black male, who ushered me into Larkin's well-appointed home. Inside, three picture windows looked directly out onto the Intracoastal where two large sailboats were heading south. It was quite a stunning view.

Larkin was seated at the head of his dining table cleaning the lenses of his glasses. He rose as I entered. "My aged eyes need all the advantages I can get," he said. "Please, sit down."

I pulled out a chair and took a seat at the corner next to him. He had been the temple's first Rabbi back in the mid-1960s and had stayed at the temple for almost 40 years until his retirement at age 70. He was now in his early 80s. His soft voice, gentle demeanor, and sincere interest in people exuded from his every pore and endeared him to all he met.

"Thanks for seeing me. I hope I didn't disrupt any plans you may have had with your wife."

"No, no. She's at the hospital having her chemo treatment. I'm all yours for the next hour."

"I'm sorry. I didn't know she was ill."

"Two bouts of cancer, this time in the pancreas. But Yahweh has spared her; for this we are most grateful. Now, how can I help you?" He replaced his glasses and stared at me with hazel eyes.

"You don't mind do you?" I asked, pulling out my new digital recorder and turning it on. Without objection, I continued. "I recently was introduced to a mountain in Saudi Arabia known as Jabal al Lawz and wondered if you'd heard of it?"

Larkin's eyebrows rose in unison. "I've heard of it."

"And?"

"Some people feel that Jabal al Lawz and Jabal Maqlā, known as Burnt Mountain, are the same because of its black granite peak. The truth is there is much speculation about where the original Mt. Sinai is. To this day, no one knows for sure."

"But it could be Jabal al Lawz."

"Anything's possible. Now what can I tell you about the twelve stones?"

It was clear Larkin's conversation regarding Jabal al Lawz was over. Perhaps it was for him, but it wasn't for me. I knew, however, that gathering further information about the mountain would have to wait until I reached the Middle-East. Then I'd query locals on the location of the genuine Mt. Sinai. In the meantime, I'd move on to the real reason I came to Larkin's.

"As I mentioned at Mort's funeral, I wanted to get your take on the twelve stones that were made into a memorial after the Israelites crossed the Jordan River . If these could be found, of what significance would they be to the Jewish people?"

Larkin leaned in and spoke in a soft voice. "Monotheism, the worship of one god, was not part of the culture back in biblical times. People worshiped many gods, so the one God of the Jews was very foreign to them. And it was understood that the God of the Jews was limited to a territory, mostly in and around Jerusalem because that's where the temple was. When you were in the city, you were under Adonai's, God's, protection. The significance of the stones is that wherever the stones were placed it would mean that land was protected by God. That's why Jews place stones at the graves of their loved ones to signify that God is there. To find the twelve stones again would not only prove that the Exodus occurred, but that God's protection of the Jewish people would be there as well."

"So, finding the stones would be a big deal to Israel?"

"Yes."

"And they could be placed back at the Jordan River where they were originally or somewhere else, I assume, and that land would have God's protection?"

"Yes, in theory."

"That would be quite a change for the Jewish people, wouldn't it? I mean, if you look at history, it doesn't seem like God protected them very well. More than six million were annihilated at the hands of the Nazis in the Holocaust. And they are still persecuted by their neighboring countries and others to this day."

"That is true."

"So, where has God's protection been?"

"It resided in the Temple and in the twelve stones. After all, the Temple no longer stands and the stones certainly aren't by the Jordan River anymore."

My brows jumped up at this revelation and my body tingled as though I'd been struck by lightning. I had merely thought of the twelve stones as a way to substantiate the Exodus, but Larkin was equating them with God's protection of the Jewish people. Could their existence be both?

"I hope, however," Larkin continued, "that the stones are never found."

My eyes widened; I was stunned by this revelation.

"Why would you say that?"

"Because Jews have been persecuted long enough. If the twelve stones were found and placed back at the river or taken somewhere else and displayed, it would create the impression that the Jewish religion is superior to all other religions and persecution of the Jews would escalate. If I knew where the twelve stones were, I would destroy them or bury them where no one could find them. The Jewish people have always had a difficult time of it, and the stones would only exacerbate the disparaging mindset of those who already hate us. It would be chaos."

"But that doesn't make sense. Wouldn't the twelve stones protect the Jewish people?"

"Only in the area designated by the stones, and who knows for sure how large that area would be? Would it be the size of a city, a country, a region? How many people could that territory hold? Thousands? Hundreds of thousands? Millions? And what would happen to the rest of the Jewish population? They would suffer terribly."

I was taken aback. What Larkin just said put quite a different slant on the situation. I'd seen the twelve stones as merely a way to prove that the Exodus took place and discover just how they were connected to Mort's death. But he saw it as potential world chaos. It struck me that perhaps that's how The Consigned saw it too and the reason why they were so interested in rendering aid.

Rabbi Larkin and I spoke a bit longer, and while I enjoyed my time with him, I left with more questions than answers. Yet, I felt more determined than ever to unravel this mystery.

Chapter 10

I called ahead and made an appointment with Helen. Her condo, the Addison North, was directly on the beach in Boca Raton just south of Camino Real and was built on land formerly known as the Arvida Beach Club. This prestigious plot of ocean front property was, in its early days, a private beach club for those individuals who purchased Arvida property west of Boca Raton. It had a pavilion, cooking grills, a life guard, and several hundred yards of pristine sand and beachfront. In its former days, many a late night cookout and party was held there as well as ocean-side nuptials.

Arvida, the name given to a residential development company owned by and made up of the initials of the late aluminum magnate Arthur Vining Davis, was responsible for multiple developments in the South Florida area. Selling residential units was paramount to the Arvida Corporation in the Boca Raton area during the 1970s and 1980s and having access to the Arvida Beach Club was tempting bait for prospective buyers. But when the properties sold out, the beach club became prime real estate for upscale condos, thus, the twin ten-story condos Addison North and South.

I parked in a guest spot in the front of the building at road level and made my way to the entrance. The landscaping, coffered to perfection, was as carefully designed as the building with lush palms, ferns, hedges, and blooming bushes accenting the entrance. In the well-appointed lobby with several living room style seating areas, a concierge desk took up a prominent location to catch visitors and residents alike upon entering or exiting the building. Cindy, the attendant, called Helen on the house phone and announced my arrival.

I took the marble lined elevator to the tenth floor. Two penthouse units took up the entire space. Helen's was one of them, located at the north end of the building. The other, I assumed a mirror image, was situated on the south end.

"Ah, Mr. Baker. So good to see you again." Helen stepped aside allowing me to enter the apartment.

"Please, call me Shea," I said as I stepped into the foyer of the open-concept dwelling. I don't know what I expected in the way of décor, maybe something quite traditional because of Helen's age. Instead, the spry little lady surrounded herself with very contemporary Danish-style furniture and bright area rugs. Large oils splashed with vivid colors in nondescript patterns graced several of the walls.

"My husband lived in the present," said Helen noticing my surprise. "He wanted us to be surrounded by optimism and hope, that's why we chose such modern furnishings. It makes me happy to wake up in such vibrant surroundings." Helen smiled as she looked around her large spacious dwelling. "Let's sit on the porch, shall we?"

The long rectangular porch wrapped around the corner of the building and had a spectacular view of the Atlantic to the north, east, and south. Northern Boca Raton including A1A could be seen all the way to the Boca Raton Hotel. To the south, the beach seemed endless.

The sun, now past its zenith, focused its warmth on the front of the building leaving the porch in shade. A pleasant sea breeze cooled us as Helen poured ice-laden sweet tea flavored with mint. It was delicious and tasted like the hot tea I was served in the Jerusalem café during my kidnapping on my first religious escapade.

"I know you didn't come here to talk about the view, so how can I help you?" Helen smiled and her eyes matched the blue-green of the ocean.

"Well, I was hoping you could enlighten me. After our conversation at Mort's funeral, I did a bit of research on those interred and inurned in the mausoleum. Quite frankly, I don't see anything in these statistics that would raise alarm."

"Really? What about the fact that a goodly number of elderly members have died off recently?"

"Their ages and death rates are consistent with the national norm."

"What about the fact that more people are being buried in the mausoleum each year?"

"That doesn't seem out of proportion either given an aggressive marketing campaign. Success builds over time." I paused and took a breath. "I'm really sorry, Helen, but I don't have anything to go on."

Helen brought her index finger to her cheek and tapped it. "There's got to be something. Cause of death?"

"Well, most of those buried in the mausoleum died of natural causes—cancer, stroke, heart attack, or in car or home accidents—except for Mort, of course. Other than that, there was a young man who was killed while riding his bicycle along A1A. There was heavy fog that morning, the driver didn't see him, and was never charged. He was hit by a—" I thumbed through my notes to find the man's name. "Erwin Schloss."

At this, Helen sat upright and her eyes grew wide. "Erwin Schloss. You're sure?"

"That's what my notes say. Why?"

"Erwin Schloss was a member of the original Mausoleum Committee. After extensive negotiations, the only way the city would go along with the temple's plans was to lease the land to the temple for an annual fee, but the temple had to raise the money for construction on their own. The city didn't put in one dime. Erwin Schloss, along with Mort Saul and two others, put up a substantial amount of their own money to get the mausoleum off the ground. What wasn't covered by their loan to the temple was borrowed from the bank. I'm not sure, but I think their agreement called for complete pay back within five years. I know for a fact, the temple hadn't sold enough crypts or niches by that time to pay them off, and so the bank loan was renegotiated and the personal loans extended."

"Now, that's putting your money where your mouth is."

"Yes, but the men weren't too happy about not getting their money back, at least six million dollars, I heard. I also heard several years ago that Erwin had to declare personal bankruptcy. Apparently he was among those who were swindled by Miami Ponzi scheme con artist Scott Rothstein. He lost a lot of his money, and he and his wife had to move out of their upscale condo and downsize into one more affordable. Maybe he's bumping off these folks to try to get his money back." Helen arched her grey eyebrows above the rims of her glasses.

"That's a little farfetched, don't you think?" I liked Helen, but Erwin Schloss running down a young man on a bicycle so the temple could sell a crypt and he could get his money back seemed a bit of a stretch for me.

Helen leaned in. The smile had left her lips. "Look, Shea, I know something is going on. Just too many of my friends are dying and most weren't close to calling it quits. Sure, they had their medical issues, but nothing close to the end of the line. The only group benefiting from so many burials is the group that put up the money in the first place. They've got to be overjoyed. Except for Mort, of course, since he's dead. Selling crypts and niches means bringing in cash to payback those who lent their own money to the project. I definitely think something's fishy here."

Maybe Helen and Stella were right. Maybe people were dying to get into the mausoleum. And, perhaps, they were having a little help. But I had nothing to go on.

"Helen, at Mort's interment you indicated that you were afraid, that your life may be in danger. Do you still feel that way?"

Helen looked down at her glass of tea and fingered her sprig of mint.

"I think any older person who hasn't yet bought a crypt is in danger."

"But you bought a crypt, didn't you?"

"As a member of the Mausoleum Committee I bought a crypt for myself because Norman already had two burial plots for us up north where our family is. But when we became temple members and watched the mausoleum being built, we decided to be buried there. It just made more sense."

"So you bought a second crypt?"

"Actually, no. When Norman died, he was buried in my crypt. I just haven't gotten around to purchasing another one for myself."

"So, you think you're a prime target as far as these men are concerned?"

"Yes," she said softly. Then she leaned in once again. Her curious eyes, topped by raised eyebrows, found mine. "By any chance when you did your research did you consider cross referencing those who had purchased crypts prior to their death with families who purchased crypts for the deceased after their death? I mean, the investors aren't really interested in those who have already purchased. They're looking for new fish to fry, people who would buy after death and could put more revenues into the coffer. If the preponderance of those who died and were placed in the mausoleum over the past few years hadn't already purchased, wouldn't that support my theory?"

I sat back, pondering her question. It was a scenario I hadn't considered.

"You do have a point. I'll look into it, but I'll need your help. I'd need a list of names and purchase dates to cross reference against the those on our buried list and their date of death. Since you're still on the Mausoleum Committee you should be able to get that."

"Playing sleuth isn't my gig," Helen said, "but I'll try."

With that decided, I told Helen I would get back to her after she had obtained the list and Stella and I had the opportunity to look it over and run it against the information we already had. I knew it would take Helen a week or two to obtain the information, and with my upcoming trip I'd be crunched for time to do anything with the information before I left. While my intention was to delve into this intriguing mystery at the temple, I wondered if I shouldn't just turn this whole thing, Helen included, over to Detective Warren so I could concentrate on my primary concern: Who killed Mort, why, and what his death had to do with the twelve stones?

I called Stella the next day and told her of my conversation with Helen. I asked her to stand by for the forthcoming information. In the meantime, Rosa and I began preparing for our upcoming trip: overseas cell phone numbers, correct adaptors for our electronics, purchasing clothes and necessities for the digs and sightseeing trips, and packing. My last trip to Jerusalem was several years ago and that one came in such a tight timeframe all I had time to do was throw my clothes into a suitcase. With this trip and Rosa going along, it took considerably more planning. She developed a checklist of all the incidentals one forgets to pack: toothbrush, ibuprofen, band aids, reading glasses, etc.

As anticipated, Helen got me the list the day before we departed. I didn't have time to look at it and simply scanned it and sent it on to Stella and asked her to do the comparisons. I'd call her from Jerusalem once we arrived to get her analysis of the information. Then I'd decide what to do with it.

Chapter 11

Our eleven hour flight on which Rosa and I read, slept, talked, and watched movies was uneventful, and we arrived in Tel Aviv having crossed multiple time zones. I knew from my previous trip that it would take our biological time clocks several days to become acclimated, and that would be just in time for us to return to Florida ten days later to adjust all over again. The best thing to do today was get to Jerusalem, check in at the hotel, look around the city for a little bit, and go to bed early.

Belinsky had a taxi waiting for us at the airport to transport us to Jerusalem, about an hour's drive away. We checked in at the Leonardo Plaza Hotel where the front office clerk handed us a note from Belinsky. He asked us to meet him and his wife for dinner in the hotel restaurant that evening. Thankfully, it was for early dining.

Belinsky had selected a table next to a picture window that looked out over the ancient city. The setting sun bathed the stucco buildings in golden hues mixed with long shadows.

"Ah, you made it." Belinsky, accompanied by his wife, Mary Anne, met us at the table. Introductions were made all around and drinks ordered.

"It's been several years since I was here last. I'd forgotten how beautiful the city is." I said.

"Yes, yes. It is beautiful, if you don't look too deep. Otherwise, it's just like any major city," Belinsky said. "It, too, has its slums and crime."

"Well, we're delighted to be here as your guests and looking forward to the dig tomorrow," Rosa said. Her eyes twinkled with the excitement of being in Israel for the first time and the adventures she would have.

"Digs tend to be hot, dusty, and mostly pot luck. Sometimes you find something of importance, but mostly it is arduous labor that produces few results. Yet, we continue to pursue them with the expectation that the next remarkable discovery is just a handful of dirt away." Belinsky smiled as he took a gulp of his Goldstar Israeli beer.

"Well, we came all this way to have the experience, and who knows maybe we'll uncover that extraordinary find after all." Rosa brimmed with enthusiasm as she sipped her Merlot.

At 5:30 a.m. the next morning, we left for Tiberias on the Sea of Galilee just over 100 miles north of Jerusalem. When we got there, the lead archeologist, Dr. Susan Silverman of Hebrew University in Jerusalem, gave us a brief history of the city. Named in honor of the Roman emperor Tiberius, it was founded by King Herod Antipas as the new capital of his kingdom in 19 CE. The current excavation that focused on the center of the ancient city, had uncovered several structures—a large colonnade, foundations of a temple to the emperor Hadrian, and a basilica. We would be working in the location of what was a bathhouse.

After receiving instructions from Silverman, we toiled alongside Belinsky and others under a small tent, open on all sides. We carefully used trowels and paint brushes to scrape and brush away dirt in a shallow trench. We took a thirty minute break mid-morning for cold sandwiches and fruit, and by two o'clock we were tired, dirty, and ready for a substantial meal. The dig didn't render any extraordinary finds; nevertheless, we had the experience of a lifetime working alongside the notable archeologist, her assistants, the professor, and speaking to them about their work. I was able to begin my assignment for the magazine by photographing the professor with his students and Simone Coffee, Belinsky's thesis winner. Tomorrow, I would take more photos and interview others. Then I would begin writing the article.

As our second day dawned, Rosa was feeling the time warp big time so I went to the dig alone. She would sleep in, then take in the sights of the notable city later in the morning. We agreed to meet back at the hotel around 4 p.m. I found her on the porch with a glass of wine looking over the ancient city. I planted a kiss on her cheek.

"How was it today?" she asked.

"Pretty much the same as yesterday—hot and dusty." I grabbed a beer from the suite fridge and took a seat next to Rosa on the porch. It was good to be looking at the green city park below us instead of the dust of the ancient ruins. "But someone did find several ceramic beads, and that sent everyone into ecstasy. I was able to get some great photos, so from that perspective it was a successful day. It's refreshing to see such excitement over finding such a small object. How was your day? Make a dent in our credit card?"

"Just a little one," said Rosa, indicating a small space between her thumb and index finger. "But I hit the jackpot at the museum and uncovered one of those extraordinary finds we spoke about at dinner last night."

I braced myself for the thought that she had purchased an expensive ancient artifact that would do nothing but take up space and collect dust on our bookshelf. But, I reminded myself that Rosa was a prudent and frugal shopper. We didn't have any credit card debt and the few bills we had were always paid on time. Our motto had always been "Live below your means," so I rested easy in the personal finances department and knew if she had purchased something extraordinary, it wouldn't break the bank.

"So what did you buy?"

"Buy? No, no. I didn't buy anything," said Rosa. "It was given to me for free."

"So bring it out here and let me see what this prized piece is." Rosa had me hooked.

"It's not something tangible, Shea; it's intangible. It's information."

I struggled to see what kind of free information was so valuable that she equated it with winning a jackpot.

"Go on," I urged.

"I went to the Israel Museum and was looking at an ancient ossuary that had been uncovered on a dig many years ago when an older gentleman came up and started a conversation. He told me all about the piece as though he had an intimate knowledge of it. When we finally got around to introducing ourselves, I realized his name was the same as the one listed on a placard next to the ossuary. He was the archeologist who discovered it. He works for the museum. His name is Misha Rueben."

The name didn't mean anything to me, but as she explained her chance encounter, she hit me with the theoretical million dollar jackpot.

"When he found out we lived in South Florida and I told him Deerfield Beach was next to Boca Raton, he asked me to have coffee with him in the museum café. After we sat down, he told me that he knew of only one person in Boca and asked me, on a long shot, if I knew him. Guess who it was?"

"Don't have a clue," I said, taking a swig of beer.

"Mort Saul."

I spewed beer all over the balcony, her response having hit me like a blow to the gut. I wiped foam off my already dirty shirt and gathered my composure.

"Mort Saul? How does he know Mort?"

"He doesn't. Never met him. He only knows *of* him."

"But how? What's the connection?"

"I don't really know. He was most reluctant to give me any more information but certainly wasn't shy about grilling me about how we knew him. I told him it was you who knew him and he told me he wanted to meet you."

"Did you tell him Mort was dead?"

"I figured you could tell him that." Rosa handed me Reuben's business card. "He said to call him the minute you get back. He wants to meet you tomorrow at the museum."

My head swirled with questions as I dialed his number. How did he know Mort? Did he have information that could lead me to his killer? What could he tell me about the twelve stones? After I made an appointment to meet

Reuben at the museum when we returned from the dig tomorrow, I phoned Stella to see if she finished analyzing the information I gave her.

"Hi Boss." Her voice was as perky as always. "Having a good time?"

"As good as one can digging in the dirt. Making any progress on the list I gave you?"

"Well . . . that list certainly was interesting. I cross referenced all the people who had died and been buried in the Mausoleum over the past ten years and what I discovered may just support Helen's theory."

"Shoot," I said. I'd already had one surprise today, what was one more?

"It seems there is nothing remarkable to report up until about three years ago. Then the number of people being buried in the mausoleum who didn't pre-purchase crypts begins to climb. So Helen may be right. Temple members just may be dying to get into the mausoleum."

Stella had uncovered some fascinating information. I wanted to tell Helen but it would have to wait until I got back to Florida. Then I would consider turning the entire mystery over to Detective Warren. In the meantime, I had Mort's killer on my mind. To move that case forward, I needed to speak with Misha Reuben and see how he was connected to Mort

Chapter 12

In the waning afternoon light, I could see an older man hunched and unsteady pacing back and forth on the landing in front of the museum. Rosa had described Reuben to me, so I felt sure this man was him.

"Hi, I'm Shea Baker. Are you by any chance Misha Reuben?"

"I am," said the man almost quivering.

I stuck out my hand in greeting but was dumbstruck when he grabbed me and gave me a bear hug instead. His slight frame shook against my chest.

"Please forgive me," he said releasing me. "You don't know what this means and how excited I am to meet you. It is obvious that Yahweh has brought us together." He pointed an index finger toward heaven and spoke in a thick Israeli accent. His eyes twinkled as he spoke.

"I'm afraid I don't know what this is all about."

"Come, come," he said. "I'll explain it all to you. And, please, call me Misha."

Without a word, I followed his slow gait down a series of wide halls in the museum, then through a pass coded and voice recognition security door marked "Employees Only." On the other side, he led me down another sequence of halls to a door with his name on the outside. He withdrew a set of keys from his pocket and fumbled with them until he found the select one. When he tried to slip it into the lock, however, his shaking hands let loose of the keys and they clattered to the floor sending an echo down the corridor. He looked around furtively as though someone might be watching. All the while, a string of security cameras recorded our every move.

I picked up the keys and handed them back to Misha. No need to mention his apparent infirmity.

"Parkinson's," he offered as he unlocked the door.

When he turned on the light, it lit up a small office unlike any I'd ever seen—no clutter, no knick knacks. It was amazingly spotless with everything precisely spaced on his desk and bookshelves.

"Please, take a seat." Misha gestured to one of the guest chairs opposite his desk. He took a seat in a plush leather swivel chair behind his neat desk opposite me.

"What's this all about?" I asked once we were both settled.

"I don't know where to begin," he said in a trembling voice. "Perhaps it's best that I show you something." He fished into his pants pocket, took out his wallet and opened it. From under a flap behind his money he took out a piece of paper. He carefully unfolded it and slid it across the desk toward me. "Read it," he said.

I picked up the well-creased note. In scribbled handwriting it read, B*oca Raton, Florida. Mort Saul.* A gasp of recognition escaped my lips.

"When I met your wife yesterday, I had no idea that the chance meeting would be the answer to my prayers and connect me to Mort Saul."

"I don't understand." I said. I returned the scrap of paper.

"A man gave this to me. He said this man," Misha tapped Mort Saul's name on the paper, "was the key to finding a very important artifact that I've been searching for. Thirty-five years I've been looking for this object and the man says Mort Saul knows where it is." He refolded the piece of paper and stuck it back into his wallet.

"Exactly what is this artifact?"

Misha let out a sigh. "Unfortunately, I can't tell you. But rest assured it is very valuable. Monetarily, yes, but more importantly, historically. In fact, its whereabouts could have world-wide implications."

World-wide implications. No wonder The Consigned had become involved. They only dealt in world altering events.

"And you can't tell me what this object is?"

"I'd love to, believe me. But after seeking it for so long and being so close, I don't want to jeopardize my finding it by disclosing what it is to a . . . please, I mean no offense . . . a complete stranger."

"So, what do you want from me?"

"Tell me about Mort Saul." He placed his folded hands on the desk, leaned in, and looked at me expectantly. "What kind of man is he? What does he do for a living? Anything you could tell me would be most beneficial."

"There are probably a number of Mort Sauls in South Florida," I explained. "After all, it is a fairly common Jewish name. All I can tell you is that I know *a* Mort Saul."

"That's it?"

"Well, I might be able to tell you more about the Mort Saul I know, but only in exchange for something I want."

Misha sat back. His silence, hesitation, and the wringing of his hands suggested he was weighing some heavy options.

"Well, I guess I'll be going," I said. I rose to leave.

"Wait!" Misha shouted. He motioned with his hand for me to sit back down. I did.

"Name your price," he finally said. His once warm eyes took on a cool stare.

"You're well known in this region, have lots of connections."

"I know people," he said reluctantly.

"And you've pulled strings to get things done."

"Some strings. From time to time."

I leaned forward and looked Misha straight in the eyes.

"I want to go to Jabal al Lawz."

Misha's eyebrows shot above his glasses like a rocket and his mouth dropped open.

"Jabal al Lawz! Why?"

"It's a long story. Let's just say that if you want more information about Mort Saul, you'll need to get me to the mountain first."

Misha stood up abruptly, adjusted his glasses and unsteadily paced behind his desk.

"Getting you to the mountain is impossible. It's in Saudi Arabia. I can't just snap my fingers and make that happen. Arrangements have to be made. Officials must be bribed. These things take time." He placed his hands on his desk, leaned toward me and eyed me with suspicion. "Besides, I'd need a little more from you about Mort Saul to prove that you have information I need before I'd go to the trouble to arrange your passage to Jabal al Lawz."

I took a long shot. "Twelve stones."

Misha stood before me bewildered, silent. His hunched frame seemed to contract onto itself until his stature became little more than that of a gnome.

"How long do I have to make arrangements?" he asked.

"Unfortunately, I have a limited time here. Two days is all I can manage."

"Two days!"

"That's all," I said.

Misha plopped into his chair like a spent ragdoll.

"I'll see what I can do." His voice was barely audible.

Chapter 13

The next day Rosa and I continued the dig with Belinsky and the students. In the evening, we ate in a wonderful little restaurant not far from the hotel, then I started my article. The following morning I continued to write and sort through photos I'd taken from the dig and select the ones for the article. With only a few hours left of the afternoon to ourselves, Rosa and I took in several historic sites in the city—Via Dolorosa, the path that Jesus walked on the way to his crucifixion, and the Western Wall, what is left of the limestone wall of the Old City of Jerusalem, a revered Jewish site. We then returned to the hotel.

Despite all the diversions, waiting to hear back from Misha was nerve racking. Not just because of the two day wait, but because I wondered if I had done the right thing. I had never resorted to using pressure to get what I wanted, but then again, no one had ever needed something from me so bad that I had an actual bargaining chip.

Evidence. That word rang loud and clear in my ears. Professors Belinsky and Clark and even Pastor Powell had all said the same thing—without evidence, no one can prove the Exodus took place. I now had the opportunity to see for myself if Jabal al Lawz was where the Israelites camped for so long. Maybe I could find something that would prove it happened and see where the Israelites crossed the Jordan River. Perhaps that would help me understand the mystery of the twelve stones surrounding Mort's death. All this was motive enough to try to go on this unorthodox road trip, but my biggest concern was Rosa. What would I tell her if Misha was able to get me to the mountain? How'd I tell her I'd be gone for two days without her? Just as I considered all these questions, the phone rang.

"The arrangements have been made," said Misha. "Meet me at the Museum tomorrow morning at seven a.m." His voice sounded agitated and he hung up before I could respond.

Now it was time for me to face the music with Rosa. I wasn't looking forward to it. Fortunately the next phone call resolved the dilemma for me.

"Mary Anne just called and asked me on a two day trip to Tel Aviv, just the two of us. Her sister lives there and we'd be staying at her home. You'll be at the dig and this would be a good way for me to get to know her better and see the city. Do you mind, Shea?" Rosa looked at me expectantly.

This couldn't have been set up more perfectly if I had planned it myself.

"What about your wanting to keep an eye on me?"

"I think Professor Belinsky can do that for me and keep you out of trouble while I'm away. Besides, you saw the city during your escapade with the cloak, but I haven't. It's only fair that I have a chance to do that, after all, that's why we came. Isn't it? To see Israel?" She gave me a confident smile.

"Of course I don't mind. You go right ahead and have a good time."

"You're a gem," said Rosa, planting a kiss on my cheek. "We can stay in touch by cell." I merely nodded in agreement while she called Mary Anne to make rendezvous arrangements.

As I lay in bed that night, the true impact of what I was about to do hit me big time. Sleep was an illusion; my mind raced and my heart beat like a bass drum. I was embarking on a clandestine and illegal trip into Saudi Arabia to find evidence of the Exodus, something archeologists and historians had never had an opportunity to do. I couldn't tell Rosa about it, and no one would know where I was. Why was I doing this? Was it really Mort's death that was propelling me, or was it something bigger—my male ego? Was it too late to back down?

Rosa was up at five a.m., packed, and ready to meet Mary Anne in the lobby. I walked her down, gave her a long hug and kiss and waved goodbye. As I scooted back upstairs to pack, I was a jumble of expectation and trepidation at my upcoming journey. I didn't exactly know what I would need as I certainly didn't know what to expect, but I put together a small bag of essentials—my camera with a powerful zoom lens, binoculars, notebook and pencil, passport, cell phone, sunglasses—and stuck some money in my zippered belt. A cab dropped me off at the museum.

"All set?" asked Misha. His usually hunched form seemed much taller than when I'd left him several days ago.

"I suppose, for someone who doesn't know what to expect."

"You're the one who insisted."

His words branded my heart.

"If you were able to arrange for me to get to Jabal al Lawz, how come you never went?"

Misah's nostrils flared. "Do you think I've never wanted to go? I've tried to get there several times but I'm a bit high profile in Israel and other parts of the world. The Saudi government isn't too keen on having renowned Jews

126

on their soil., or archeologists in their deserts. We might find something."

"I'm sure there are charges for this kind of thing. How do I repay you?"

"Let's take care of that when you get back. *If* you get back." Misha looked at me and shrugged his shoulders as though it was a possibility.

"If I don't get back, you won't find out about Mort Saul," I said with resolution.

Just then, a rugged looking man approached us. He and Misha spoke in Arabic.

"This is Abdul-Jalil. He will take you where you want to go. He knows a bit of English. Listen to him and only him. Do what he says. You must pretend to be a deaf mute. Speak to him only when the two of you are alone," said Misha.

I looked at my guide. His face was rough, his eyes like dark wells. He wore a loose fitting off white shirt over baggy black pants and a sly grin under his short dark beard.

"Here," Misha continued, "rub your face with this. It will turn your skin brown and help you blend in." He handed me a can of what looked like brown shoe polish. "And here is a tunic. Put it on now and wear it always. God's speed." he shuffled away and left me with Abdul-Jalil.

"We go," he said with a deep Arabic accent. He led me to a jeep loaded with sleeping gear, a box of food, and two five gallon metal containers of gasoline.

I looked at him quizzically.

"No gas in desert."

I pasted my face and neck in brown cream while he drove and described our travel plans.

"We travel to hidden airport. Fly to Jordan. Drive to Saudi Arabia. Have four hours on mountain. In, out. Maybe no one see us." As he spoke, a toothpick bobbed up and down in his mouth.

"You've done this before?"

He held up a thumb and two fingers indicating he'd done it three times.

"So how do you know Misha?"

Abdul-Jalil threw his head back and let out a hearty laugh. "Work together."

"Doing what?"

He transitioned the tooth pick to the other side of his mouth with a flick of his tongue. "He archeologist. Me business man." His mouth curled at the corners into a sly grin.

I was smart enough to read between the lines. Misha fed him artifacts from time to time and he fenced them on the black market. Or, maybe he led Misha to great discoveries . . . for a hefty price.

My guide pointed to the cream. "Put on hands, arms, ankles. Don't forget ears," he said.

I hit all the spots he mentioned. By the time I finished, we drove into a small hard pan airport out in the middle of nowhere. I donned my sunglasses.

"Keep mouth closed," Abdul-Jalil said sternly not mincing words.

We got out of the jeep and unloaded our belongings including the gas cans. As we walked toward a small single engine plane, two men met us. They spoke to Abdul-Jalil in Arabic. I just stood there and occasionally gave a slight bow. I could see they were deep in an animated discussion like Middle-Easterners haggling over the price of something in a bazaar. Finally, Abdul-Jail scowled, then slapped their palms with some cash.

As we walked toward the plane, I realized it wasn't in the best of shape. The paint was worn—no numbers or markings—and looked as though it had been sand blasted by the strong winds of this arid climate. I wondered what the engine looked like considering the outside shell.

We transferred our gear and the gasoline cans into the cargo hold then climbed aboard. One of the men climbed into the pilot's seat; Abdul-Jalil took the co-pilot's seat. I sat in the back of the four-seater and strapped myself in. It had been years since I was in a small plane and I didn't like it one bit. I'd always been susceptible to claustrophobia and this was going to be close. My only saving grace was that the seat next to me was empty. That gave me some breathing room. If I got into real trouble, I always had my anti-anxiety medication in my pocket.

We were soon aloft, the noise from the engine excruciatingly loud. Flying low over the countryside all I could see for miles in any direction was sand except when we crossed a river. Then I could see vegetation and fertile plains where farms rose from the arid land. In the far distance beyond the farms and sand, I could see the silhouette of jagged mountain peaks rising against the blue sky. We were headed in their direction. Several hours later we landed on an obscure airstrip in the middle of nowhere. There were no buildings or signs of life. A lone jeep sat just off the makeshift runway.

The pilot kept the plane's engine running while Abdul-Jalil and I disembarked and unloaded our gear. Then the plane took off. It was on the ground less than three minutes.

"Take Jeep," said my guide.

It was hot, dusty, rattled incessantly and the vehicle had no air conditioning. I estimated the temperature somewhere in the low one hundreds with humidity around zero. Thankfully, the arid wind blew steadily through the windows and out the open hatch in the back of the jeep. If it hadn't, the strong smell of the gasoline from the cans would have overwhelmed us. The down side, however, was that the wind also covered us with fine dust that clung to our sweat soaked clothes. Bottles of water were my closest friend and I made short work of several on our ride.

"Don't drink all. Save for tomorrow."

After three hours of little chit chat with my camera pasted to my eye to document our travel, we turned off the main road onto one that looked little more than a narrow path that headed further into the desert. How Abdul-Jalil found the road was a mystery to me. The jeep bounced along nothing but a long nondescript ribbon of sand that stretched endlessly through a barren monochromatic wasteland. The land was flat initially, but began to rise as we moved farther inland. Late in the afternoon, we stopped at a small square rock block building. Openings in the walls, one on each end, served as windows. The door was nothing more than a larger opening. There were no screens or doors.

"We sleep here. Travel early. Emmm . . . maybe four hours to Jabal al Lawz."

The building looked like a way station for those traveling this route. Three old army cots lined the walls. A steel table with four wooden chairs took up space in the room's center. Another table against the fourth wall held some dented pots and pans. All were covered in a fine layer of sand indicating no one had been there recently. To relieve ourselves, we walked fifty yards from the building where we found a plank with a hole in it elevated on cement blocks. That was it. No sides, no privacy. It was the most primitive outhouse I'd ever seen.

We ate bread and cured meat along with rice and beans Abdul-Jalil cooked over a small fire in an outdoor fire pit. There wasn't a tree in sight, yet it was obvious that someone had furnished the kindling and logs. As we sat around the fire, it dawned on me that I hadn't called Rosa. I pulled out my phone, turned it on and punched number one—my short cut to her cell number.

"You see tower?" asked Abdul-Jalil splaying his hands to indicate the desolation. He smiled at my look of surprise when I realized there were no modern communications systems out here, then he doubled over in laughter.

Rosa would be frantic not hearing from me, and I'd be in the dog house . . . again. This was a situation I hadn't counted on.

"How come you agreed to take me to Jabal al Lawz?"

Abdul-Jalil withdrew a toothpick from his pocket, poked at his teeth, then let it settle in his mouth. He looked at me, held up his hand and rubbed his fingers against his thumb indicating the universally accepted language of the world—money.

"You must know a lot about this region."

"Enough," he said shrugging his shoulders.

"What do you know about the Exodus of the Jews?"

"Spent long time in desert. Should have listened to directions from wives." Abdul-Jalil smiled and broke into hefty laughter once more. I laughed too. It was funny.

"What about them crossing the Jordan River and the twelve stones?"

The smile left his face.

"Time to sleep," he said rising.

Abdul-Jalil emptied one of the five gallon gasoline cans into the jeep. Though the sun was still up, we bedded down on the cots; the powerful smell of gasoline still lingered in my nostrils. As soon as the sun descended behind the mountains, the temperature made a steep downward spiral. It seemed as equally cold at night as it was searing hot during the day. I figured the temperature dropped more than forty-five degrees and now stood somewhere around fifty. The sleeping bag felt good.

"Time to go," said Abdul-Jalil shaking me from a fitful sleep.

I blinked open and shielded my eyes from the glare of the flashlight he held on my face.

"What time is it?"

"Two. We go."

I twisted sideways and was about to slip my feet into my shoes when I was abruptly pushed away.

"Careful!" said Abdul-Jalil. I followed the beam from his flashlight that was pointed at my shoes. He picked one up and knocked the heel against the concrete floor. Nothing. Then he did the same to the other. Out popped a large black scorpion the length of my hand. He crushed it with his boot. I looked at Abdul-Jalil wide-eyed. He said nothing, as though it was common knowledge that you check your shoes before putting them on. I would certainly remember that lesson for our return trip.

Breakfast was thick black coffee and a pastry. We bound our sleeping bags, packed the jeep with our few possessions and were off. Our next stop—Jabal al Lawz

Chapter 14

It was pitch black as Abdul-Jalil guided us down the road lit only by our bouncing headlights. There were no signs, no markers, yet he periodically turned right and left as though he knew the way by heart. The building pressure in my ears indicated a steep rise in the elevation and I discerned that we were traveling up valleys between the mountains, though neither could yet be seen. As the sun rose, however, the desert came alive. The brilliant sun caressed the peaks of adjacent mountains while dark shadows hugged their feet. The contrast and changing colors—yellows, golds and reds—were breathtaking.

The terrain wasn't what one would suppose a desert to be, all sand like the Sahara. This desert was a mixture of sand, mountains, stone outcroppings, and rubble leading from the desert floor up to the higher peaks.

All of a sudden, we came to an abrupt stop. Two Bedouins on camels traveling the road walked toward us. Abdul-Jalil greeted the men and appeared to be asking directions while all pointed and gestured toward the mountains. He got back into the jeep, and the camels carried their riders away.

"Jabal Musa there." Abdul-Jalil pointed toward a tall mountain to our left.

"But we're going to Jabal al Lawz, not Jabal Musa."

"Jabal Musa mean Mountain of Moses. Jabal Musa, Jabal al Lawz the same."

I was dumbstruck. Out in the middle of nowhere, a local Bedouin called Jabal al Lawz the Mountain of Moses. Undoubtedly, generations of Bedouins had passed down this label acknowledging the remarkable presence of this mountain and for whom it was named. Goose bumps rose from my arms and neck as I realized we had just stumbled upon something of incredible significance.

The road straightened for a distance and I could see a mountain in front of us that appeared higher than the rest. Before we reached the base of the mountain, we came across a pile of enormous stones that lay in ruin. Each block must have weighed several tons, and it was obvious they had been toppled by an extraordinary force. The mass was enclosed by a six foot chain linked fence topped with barbed wire. A large wooden white sign with black writing in both Arabic and English forbid anyone to enter.

Abdul-Jalil stopped the jeep. We got out and I snapped several photos of the enclosed stones. As I made my way around the fence, I noticed carvings in several of the stones. They resembled Petroglyphs of cows I'd seen in books on ancient Egypt. I took a picture of them then took out my notebook and sketched what I saw including the mound of stones.

"Altar," said Abdul-Jalil.

Though I was not a Bible scholar by any stretch of the imagination, I recalled from my childhood days in Sunday School that when Moses went to Mt. Sinai to speak with God he was gone so long the people thought he had abandoned them. Aaron, Moses's second in command, allowed the Israelites to take matters into their own hands. He collected gold from the people, melted it, and fashioned it into a calf. The golden calf was placed on an altar and the people began worshipping it. God was not pleased.

The stones with their petroglyphs of cows suggested that this might have been that altar. After all, the Israelites lived in Egyptian captivity for centuries and assimilated, or, at the very least, were quite familiar with much of their culture and artistry including their idols. Could the mountain before me be Mt. Sinai? Was I walking on sacred ground?

When Moses eventually came down from the mountain and saw that the people had turned their backs on God and were now worshiping an idol, he was so distraught that he threw down the clay tablets on which God had written the Ten Commandments; the plaques shattered.

I walked farther from the altar inspecting the ground. Maybe there was some kind of artifact out there I could find that would prove the Israelites had actually camped there. As I milled around, I noticed an etching on a medium sized rock. Upon closer inspection, I realized the carving was the outline of a foot. As I wandered further, I saw another foot, then another. Who had carved these images and why? I was taking photos of the rocks when I heard Abdul-Jalil call from the jeep.

"We go," he said pointing at his watch. I knew we were on a tight schedule so I returned to the jeep wishing I could spend days instead of hours walking the land.

As we got closer to the mountain, its peak appeared black as though in shadow, yet the sun was shining bright. We took a left, curved around the base of the mountain, and came out on the other side. Abdul-Jalil came to a stop. He pointed at an obscure path that led up the mountain.

"Four hours up, down." He looked at his watch and indicated what time I had to be back.

I placed my nonworking cell phone in the glove box, grabbed my knapsack packed with my belongings—notebook and pencil, passport, camera, binoculars, and water—and began my ascent. Abdul-Jalil stayed with the jeep. It was an arduous climb over jagged granite rocks and it took me an hour to reach the top, including stops to hydrate and catch my breath in the thinning air. As I emerged onto the peak, the entire area appeared burned as though an incredibly hot fire had singed a large portion of the mountain. I could also see a distinct line in the granite where the black portion of the mountain stopped and the natural pinkish-brown granite began. The delineation was as distinct as day and night.

I picked up a rock and inspected it. It, too, appeared charred. Using a larger rock, I broke a point off the smaller one. Inside, the granite was pinkish-brown like the rest of the mountain and those surrounding it; yet, the outside of the tip was shiny and black as coal. What had happened on the mountain to cause such a phenomenon? I snapped photos of the peak and rock then placed it in a plastic zip bag and put it in my knapsack.

Standing atop the mountain, I was struck by the awesome but barren view. As far as I could see in every direction there was nothing but jagged granite mountain peaks, outcroppings of rocks, and sand. I wondered how the Israelites did it, how they survived in this desolate terrain for forty years?

I looked down at the Jeep and Abdul-Jalil. Both appeared miniscule. I walked across the summit of the mountain and scanned its base on the opposite side with my binoculars. That's where I spied a v-shaped rock structure. The walls appeared shoulder high of stacked stone and funneled from an open area toward the base of the mountain. It reminded me of a chute; something that would herd sheep or goats to a specific location. Close to the chute were round objects like circular sections of columns that when stacked together once stood upright. It was evident that the columns had collapsed, scattering their sections. Someone had built these structures, but was it the Israelites? If so, what did they use them for? I didn't have time to inspect more carefully, so I took out my notebook, sketched the structure and took several photos zooming in. I wondered if the same force that had toppled the alter had also thrown down the columns.

Scanning the adjacent land, my binoculars picked up a gigantic dark grey rock that stood vertically atop an outcropping some distance away. While the area had numerous outcroppings, this was the only one in the entire area with a monolith. It stood out like a sore thumb against the desert. It was difficult to get a fix on just how big the rock was but it looked several stories tall. I took more photos zooming in.

By the time I had inspected the top of the mountain, made sketches of the ruins and taken photos, almost an hour and a half had elapsed. I wanted to see if we could drive to the outcropping to get a closer look at the tall rock, so I began my descent knowing it would take me about forty minutes.

Three quarters of the way down, a distant object caught my eye. I focused my binoculars on it. A military vehicle moving rapidly between two mountains was heading in our direction. I escalated my descent, slipping and sliding part of the way.

As I got closer to the jeep, I called and signaled Abdul-Jalil, but he was nowhere to be seen. When I finally got to the vehicle, I found him asleep inside.

"Someone's coming!" I said shaking him awake. The vehicle wasn't yet within sight, but I knew it was only a matter of time before it rounded the mountain. I ran around the vehicle tossed my knapsack inside and jumped in.

Abdul-Jalil grabbed my knapsack, ran to the back of the jeep and opened the hatch. I could hear him fiddling with the gas cans.

"What are you doing?" I yelled. "Someone's coming. Let's go!" I'd never been more emphatic or anxious.

Just as Abdul-Jalil hopped into the driver's seat, the military vehicle roared past us. Plumes of dust billowed into the scorching air as it screeched to a stop in front of us blocking our escape. Two men in military uniforms sporting automatic rifles jumped out and rushed both sides of our vehicle. They yanked open the doors and pulled us out.

I was patted down by a soldier with a long scar across his left cheek and whose uniform was worn and threadbare. He confiscated my notebook which I had tucked into the pocket of the tunic. Then I was barraged with questions—all in Arabic. When I didn't answer, the soldier backhanded me. The sudden and unexpected impact sent me reeling to the ground. As I lifted my head, I noticed a red patch in the sand. I drew the sleeve of my tunic across my nose; blood left a trail down the cloth.

I figured that an assignment in this remote location was probably reserved for the dregs of the Saudi army and their finding something or someone out of the ordinary was merely a diversion from the oppressive boredom of a regular day. Play toys. That's what we were.

Pushing myself up to a sitting position, I pleaded with my eyes and gestured as well as I could with my hands that I could not hear or speak. When Scarface realized he'd get nowhere with me, he grabbed my arm, jerked me from the sand, and shoved me to the other side of the jeep where he and his partner could concentrate on Abdul-Jalil.

While I was unable to understand what they said, it appeared that Scarface was demanding our documents. Sweat beaded my brow as I thought about my passport in the pocket of my knapsack. If they found that and the American that had snuck into their country unlawfully, I'd be dead meat.

Abdul-Jalil reached into his pocket and produced two papers. As Scarface inspected them he leered at us while his accomplice pointed his rifle at our mid sections. It reminded me of the last time I was in the Middle-East and had been kidnapped at gun point. It was all I could do to hold it together.

Moments later, Scarface handed the papers back to Abdul-Jalil who said very little except when asked. Then he went to the back of our Jeep and opened the hatch. I could hear him rummaging around and felt certain he'd find my knapsack. Sure enough, he rounded the jeep carrying it. What were once beads of sweat lining my brow had now become full blown rivulets that marched down my cheeks.

Scarface placed my knapsack on the hood of the Jeep, opened it and stuck his hand inside. Out came my binoculars. He placed them to his eyes and focused from mountain to mountain. He showed the field glasses to his colleague who did the same then placed them on the hood of the vehicle.

Next Scarface withdrew my camera. He looked at it, played with the zoom lens, even took a photo of his fellow soldier pointing his automatic at Abdul-Jalil and myself. It was placed on the hood of the jeep as well. I stood there as calm as I could muster while I seethed inside. There went my photos and any proof that Jabal al Lawz might have been Mt. Sinai, not to mention twelve hundred dollars of my hard earned money. I figured the optical devices would become the least of my worries, however, for at any moment they would locate my passport.

To my surprise, however, Scarface never inspected the knapsack more thoroughly. After another lively discussion between the two soldiers with some laughter thrown in, Scarface stuck the binoculars and camera back into the knapsack and placed it in their vehicle. He then returned to our Jeep, grabbed our sleeping bags and what little food stuffs we had left and tossed them into his vehicle as well. He made one last trip to our jeep and extracted the full gas can, leaving us the empty one and a distinct smirk.

Next, he strode over to me and put his face but inches from mine. His dark green eyes inspected me. He smelled like desert dust mixed with old sweat and his hot breath, emitting an odor like a sewer, made me wince. He took his thumb and pressed it hard into my cheek smearing a line of blood and sweat from my ear to my chin. He looked at his thumb, at me, back at his thumb. I held my breath. I prayed he hadn't wiped off my faux brown skin.

Rosa flashed through my mind. I had put her through hell once before and now I was doing it again. What was I thinking?

Suddenly, I felt a sharp blow. My legs crumpled, and white, red and green stars danced before my eyes.

Then my world went black.

Chapter 15

I awoke in the passenger's seat of the rumbling jeep. Blood stained my tunic, my head throbbed unmercifully, and I could hardly breathe. I touched my aching nose and found two small pieces of blood soaked cloth packed in each nostril. Wanting to see the damage, I turned the rear view mirror around; a grotesque face stared back at me. My right eye, almost swollen shut, was beginning to blacken as was my left. My nose was crooked, my lips lacerated, red and twice their size, and my cheeks inflamed. Dry blood and sand crusted my face and neck. With no stretch of anyone's imagination, I was unrecognizable. I opened my mouth to speak and excruciating sharp pain shot through my head. A few teeth felt loose.

"What happened?" I groaned.

"Broken nose, maybe cheek," Abdul-Jalil said. He drove at an accelerated pace as he maneuvered around the mountains.

I slumped back in my seat and closed my eyes. Scarface and his fellow thieving soldier earned more than my usual three demerits reserved for those who committed the most egregious offenses.

We reached the way station without further incident. Abdul-Jalil helped me from the Jeep into the structure and sat me on a cot. My face was so painful I thought I would heave right on the spot. In my condition, however, that would have been a disaster. Who knows how many teeth would have come up with the pastry from the morning?

My throat was parched, I needed water. Thankfully, my astute guide had stashed several gallons of it under one cot before we left for Jabal al Lawz, otherwise I was sure the light-fingered soldiers would have taken them too. I tried to drink from a tin cup, but touching it to my lips only brought tears to my eyes. I had to hold it up, tip my head back and try to hit a narrow bullseye between my split and partially opened lips. As the water went down, the taste of blood went with it.

Abdul-Jalil said little as he doused a cloth with water and tried to wipe the blood from my face and neck. Just the touch of the fabric on my skin brought excruciating pain.

"You sleep," he said. He took the third cot apart and draped the canvas over me. It wouldn't be the warmth of the sleeping bag as the temperature dropped, but it was all we had. It would be a cold night for me, colder still for Abdul-Jalil.

When I awoke the next morning, I checked my shoes then went outside. Abdul-Jalil had built a fire and made coffee from grounds that had spilled in the back of the Jeep from the food stuffs the soldiers had taken. It was weak and bitter, but it was all we had. I still hurt like the dickens and my whole face was tender to the touch. My teeth, however, seemed a bit more secure and I could open my mouth more easily.

"What happens now?" I asked.

"Return," replied Abdul-Jalil.

"Please tell me what happened."

Abdul-Jalil looked at me and let out a sigh. "Arabs different from Americans. Great shame in being . . . how you say . . . disabled. Soldier not like you because you deaf, no talk. He hit you with bottom of rifle. I hear crack; run to help. He hit me. We both on ground, guns pointed at us. I think we die. Then, two men come. They tell soldiers 'let us go.' They give soldiers money; help me get you to jeep. Tell us to leave."

"Who were the other men?"

"Not soldiers," he said.

His story was curious. Who were these anonymous men who came out of nowhere and paid the soldiers to let us live? The only answer I could come up with was The Consigned. Their reach was long and it had been my experience that they always showed up at the most unexpected times. Maybe this was one of those.

"What about my passport and the papers you showed the soldiers?"

"Passport?" He shrugged indicating he had no clue where it was. "Two papers. One mine. One yours. Yours fake."

"Thank you," I said. Abdul-Jalil gave me a slight nod.

We left the way station and headed back to the airport, no doubt riding on fumes. At each transfer, Abdul-Jalil made a point of taking along the empty gas can. Why he had such an attachment to the container I had no idea. Finally, we made it back to the museum where we met Misha.

"You look awful," he said inspecting my face. "You need a doctor."

"So it seems," I responded.

"I will take you. You can't go back to Rosa looking like this."

"I need to call her. I'm sure she's frantic with worry about where I've been and why I didn't call her."

"You chose your path. I did what I could to cover for you. Whatever the consequences, you'll have to deal with them," Misha said.

He paid Abdul-Jalil, but before my guide left, he handed me the gas can. I'm sure he saw the big question mark on my face.

"Souvenir," he said. His toothpick bobbed up and down with his words and he grinned at me upon leaving. What I was going to do with this gas can was anyone's guess, but it must have been important to Abdul-Jalil for me to have it so I carried it to Misha's car. On my way to the hospital, I phoned Rosa.

"Hi, it's me. How was your trip to Tel Aviv?" Though I felt like a wrung wash cloth, I was hoping my upbeat tone might diffuse the fireworks I knew would come.

"Shea, where are you? Are you all right?" Rosa's tone was sharp but concerned.

"It's a long story. I should be back in about two hours. I'll explain it all then. I love you." I didn't give her time to respond or ask more questions.

At the hospital they sutured my cuts, reset my nose, and cleaned me up as best they could. The important thing was I was alive and my face would heal albeit a few scars and crooked nose. It was the relationship with my beloved wife that I wondered if I had damaged beyond repair.

Misha escorted me to the door of the hotel suite. We must have looked like an odd pair—an elderly man with an unsteady gait escorting me with a face that looked like raw meat left out too long. I felt like I looked and was so doped up with painkillers that walking or thinking straight was an illusion. I took a deep breath when we got to the door of the suite.

"Don't forget our bargain. I get you to Jabal al Lawz, you tell me about Mort Saul. I'll expect you at the museum day after tomorrow."

"I'll be there," I said.

Rosa opened the door, took one look at me, and let out a loud gasp. Thankfully, all she did was get me into bed and let me sleep. I knew Mount Vesuvius would erupt when I awoke.

The next morning I stumbled into the small sitting room around 10:00 a.m. Rosa was out on the balcony reading a magazine and taking in the view.

"How long did I sleep?" I asked poking my head out the door. Rosa jumped upon hearing my voice.

"Fifteen hours," she said. "Come have a seat. I'll get you something to eat. I'm sure you're hungry."

Hungry? I had no idea the last time I had something to eat and really wasn't sure I could chew.

"Misha says neither your cheek or jaw is broken, just badly bruised, but you do have a broken nose and the cuts. He said he'd see you tomorrow."

Mt. Vesuvius appeared calm right now, but I knew the hot magma was just below the surface. Soon it would rise to the top.

I sat down while Rosa left for the kitchenette and returned with some Jell-O, applesauce, and yogurt, food I could eat without chewing. I supposed soft foods would be my diet for a few days until my face healed. That was okay by me, I could stand to lose a few pounds anyway. I spooned the food in silence waiting for my much deserved chastisement in Spanish. When it didn't come, I took Rosa's hand.

"I'm sorry Rosa for putting you through this. I just hope you can forgive me." I had no expectations of her acceptance.

Rosa looked at my bruised and bandaged face and spoke in a calm deliberate tone as though she was holding back the eruption.

"There's no doubt I'm both furious at you and relieved, Shea. After all our years together and what you put me through chasing your other mysteries, I thought you had learned your lesson about going on clandestine missions, even to help a friend. Apparently not." Tears welled in her eyes as she continued.

"What hurt most is that you didn't trust me enough to tell me about it. Not that I wouldn't have tried to stop you. When I didn't hear from you I got in touch with Professor Belinsky. He told me you never showed up for the dig that day. The only other person I knew to call was Misha Reuben. He told me what you did for him. Shea, it was noble and nice of you to accommodate the elderly archeologist, but you should have trusted me enough to tell me he had sent you on such a potentially perilous errand."

I swallowed hard hoping Rosa wouldn't notice how stunned I was.

"Just what did he say?"

"That he asked you to drop off something for him on your way back to the hotel. He didn't want to go himself because the delivery was very sensitive, and he didn't want to be recognized. When you arrived at the appointed drop off site, you were assaulted. Your camera and binoculars were stolen. It's called 'tourist assault' and apparently happens quite frequently, he says."

So that was Misha's way of covering for me.

"I thought it an innocuous favor," I said. "Who could have predicted it would turn out like this?"

"Aren't you going to report the assault to the police?"

"I don't want to delay our trip home."

Rosa stood with her arms crossed over her bosom shaking her head. "What I don't understand, is why you didn't take my phone calls or call me? I was frantic."

"I wasn't able to talk," I said. "Thankfully you were able to reach Misha and he was able to tell you what happened."

"Yes, thankfully," said Rosa. "Oh, I almost forgot, Meyer and Mary Anne called. They were both very concerned about you and would like to see us before we leave."

"Please tell them I appreciate their concern, but I just don't feel up to it."

"Well, our plane leaves in a few days and we'll be back in the U.S. soon with all this behind us. I'll just tell the Belinsky's we'll see them when we return to Florida." She picked up my plate and made her way to the kitchenette. "By the way, I got rid of that awful gas can while you were sleeping. It stunk and honestly, Shea, I don't know why you even had it. What were we going to do with it?"

My countenance drooped. I certainly wasn't attached to the gas can, but still, there was something about it. Rosa returned with a plastic bag pinched between her fingers. The mild odor of gasoline scented the air.

"Here. Before they took the gas can away I found this plastic bag in it. I washed the gasoline off it the best I could. It's got something very important in it. Do you want to tell me how it got there?"

I could see my treasured passport in the bag, but it was something else altogether that brought me the most excitement—the rock from the top of Jabal al Lawz. I opened the bag, withdrew the rock and closed my hand around it.

"What's that?" asked Rosa.

"A small memento," I said.

Rosa crinkled her nose. "From your assault? That's a strange thing to keep."

Next, I took out my passport. As I thumbed through the pages, something fell to the floor. Rosa picked it up.

"Why it looks like a digital card from a camera."

All I could do is stare wide-eyed at the small object. So that's what Abdul-Jalil was doing in the back of the jeep while the soldiers bore down on us. He had removed the digital card from my camera and placed both it and my passport into the bag that held the stone then stuffed it into the empty gas can. Who would have looked there? Now I understood why he had kept the container with us throughout our return. No one would have suspected what was inside and I would be safe. If he had been in the room, I would have kissed his stubbled face.

"Funny, isn't it," said Rosa, inspecting the card, "that the men who assaulted you and stole your camera would remove the card? What robber would take the time to do that?" She stared hard at me taking on that look I was so familiar with, the unspoken one that was loud and clear: "You've lied and I've caught you in another mystery, haven't I?"

Mt. Vesuvius erupted.

The words egotistical, selfish, uncaring rang in my ears. I couldn't argue with her.

Chapter 16

When I awoke, Rosa was already up and gone. Thankfully, she had left me a note that she had gone to breakfast . . . alone. That meant she needed time to assess our discussion. In a way, that was a good sign. It meant she would weigh our twenty-eight years together against my unconfessed iniquities. Hopefully, the scale would tip in my direction.

Even though my emotions were on edge, I felt physically much better after a day of rest and ice packs plastered to my battered and bruised face, so I headed for the museum to keep my appointment with Misha. I didn't know what to expect but was certain Mort Saul's name would be front and center. He met me at the entrance and shuffled me back to his office, this time using a cane. His eyes nervously scanned the corridors and he constantly looked over his shoulder.

"Someone following us?" I asked.

"I've had a visitor." Angst permeated his tone. "Maybe you know him?"

"I doubt it. I don't know anyone in Jerusalem."

"He's not from here. He's from Boca Raton. Meyer Belinsky?"

I stopped dead. "Professor Belinsky from Florida Atlantic University?"

"The same," said Misha.

"Yes, I know him. He's the reason Rosa and I are here. He invited us on his spring break dig. I'm doing a story for a magazine on his students and him. What did he want?"

Misha looked around furtively. "In my office," he said, still eyeing the halls. He gripped my arm tightly and guided me down the corridor. He slid his pass through the scanner, spoke his name into the audio mic, and we entered the hallway to his office. "By the way you still look awful."

"I won't win a beauty contest that's for sure," I said.

Once inside Misha's office I took my usual seat across from his desk. He sat behind it with folded hands on top. A long sigh escaped his lips; he seemed relieved to have arrived safely.

"Now what about Belinsky?" I asked.

"We'll get to him," said Misha. "First you need to live up to your end of the bargain."

I took a deep breath. "Before we get started, I need a favor," I said in sheepish fashion.

A loud thud exploded into the room as Misha slammed his hands on the desk. His eyes blazed. "A favor! Haven't I done enough for you?"

I was startled by his outburst but proceeded just the same. I always operated on the old adage "nothing ventured, nothing gained."

"Yes, but this is very important. It's connected to the twelve stones." If I had been honest, I would have added the term 'loosely,' but I figured if I mentioned them I'd have a better chance of his cooperation.

He inhaled slowly gathering himself then waved a hand for me to go on.

"You have testing labs here right?"

"The best."

"I need something tested." I withdrew the rock from Jabal al Lawz and handed it to him. He looked at it curiously.

"A rock? Is this some kind of joke?"

"No joke, I assure you. I need to know what made the outside black while the inside is the typical granite color."

Without a word, Misha picked up his phone and punched in an extension. He spoke in Hebrew into the phone. In no time, a young woman arrived in a white lab coat.

"This is my assistant."

The dark haired homely-looking woman whose name badge read "Rhonda C. Frankle" nodded politely but never made eye contact.

"The 'C' on your name badge, a beautiful middle name?" I tried to make the timid woman's introduction as pleasant as possible.

"My maiden name," she said shyly.

Without further conversation, Rhonda produced a plastic bag and held it open in front of me. Once I dropped the rock into it, she zipped up the bag, turned around and left the room.

"Of course, there are lots of tests to run and the results won't be back before you leave. I'll have to send the rock back to you, and I'll email the report when it's done." A hint of a wry smile crossed his lips as though he had pulled a big one over on me. I didn't want to leave Tel Aviv without my rock, but what could I do? It was now held captive at the museum by Rhonda. I wondered if I'd ever see it again.

"Now that distractions are over," said Misha leaning back in his chair, "tell me about Mort and the twelve stones."

"There's not much to tell," I said. "The Mort Saul I knew emailed me some time ago and asked me to meet him at a mausoleum, said it was important."

Misha crinkled his nose. "You said *knew*, not *know*. Am I to take it Mort Saul is no longer with us?"

"He was murdered in the mausoleum the day we were to meet."

Misha sucked air and his face puckered. He drew his long fingers over his head. "This is not good news. Do you know what he wanted to speak to you about?"

"He referenced a Bible verse about crossing the Jordan River and the Israelites building a memorial out of twelve stones taken from the river bed. He also mentioned an article that explained there was no evidence that the Sinai desert was the location of the Exodus and therefore it hadn't really occurred."

"That's all?"

"He wanted me to bring a recorder and camera."

"Do you know why?"

"I'm assuming he wanted me to record something very important either audibly or visually. Unfortunately, he was killed before we could meet. I don't know what he wanted to tell me, but it seems logical that it had to do with the stones."

"This has got to be the same Mort Saul that was written on my note," said Misha.

"How's that?"

"Too many coincidences."

With his elbows on the desk, Misha entwined his fingers leaving his index fingers pressed together and pointing upward like the steeple of a church. He brought them to his lips, closed his eyes and appeared deep in thought. I wondered what he was thinking and how Mort's death had affected him.

"Come," he finally said, pushing himself up from his chair and grabbing his cane.

I got up and followed his unsteady walk to a door in his office different from the one I had entered. Just before I got to the door he put up his cane blocking me. He turned, stood as tall as he could muster, and eyeballed me with a stern stare. He shook his bony index finger in my direction.

"I must have your word that you will not tell a soul what I'm about to show you."

I had no idea what I was about to swear to but figured it was probably something important.

"I promise," I said making an X across my heart and holding up my right hand. I felt like a kid swearing allegiance to a secret club. On second thought, maybe I was.

I followed Misha through the door and into a large connecting room. It was packed with shelves of artifacts. I was mesmerized at the display—clay pitchers, bowls, oil lamps, statues—by the hundreds.

"Did you find all these?"

"Many, yes. Others were found by my colleagues and their students. No one sees these until the museum is ready to show them. And some will never be seen." I wondered how many others had been given to Abdul-Jalil to fence on the black market.

Misha moved to a large steel cabinet. He pulled out a ring of keys from his pants pocket, unlocked the doors, and pulled them open.

"Here, help me move these boxes to the table," he said. He lifted a square wooden box and shuffled to the table. Between the two of us, we carried eleven identical boxes to the table.

"What are these?" I asked.

"Open them," instructed Misha.

I carefully took the tops off the boxes exposing a large stone of around equal size, color and shape in each. Somehow, they reminded me of something—a recessed memory smothered in vagueness.

Misha panned the boxes with his hand. "What we have here are eleven stones from the crossing of the Jordan River." He stood resolute a wide smile on his thin lips. Tears trickled from the corners of his eyes; he soaked them up with his handkerchief.

"So, they do exist," I said gaping at the stones. I was mesmerized by the artifacts before me.

"Yes. It's taken me thirty-five years to find them. These are the only proof we have that the Israelites actually crossed the Jordan River and that the Exodus took place."

"The article that Mort and his rabbi discussed about the Exodus being bogus, it was written by Professor Belinsky. Is that why he was here? He wanted to know whether the stones really existed?"

"Yes. I denied it, of course, but he said he had proof that I had them and demanded to see them. When I refused, he told me it didn't matter whether I had them or not. No one would ever see them anyway."

"But what could he do? Isn't the museum secure?"

"Certainly, but stranger things have happened. Valuable artwork housed in supposedly secure galleries including the Louvre has been stolen, so who is to say what's secure?"

"What about Jabal al Lawz? If you had evidence that it was in fact Mount Sinai, wouldn't that be proof enough? Then you wouldn't actually need the twelve stones to substantiate the Exodus."

"That Jabal al Lawz is the true Mt. Sinai is just a myth, unless, of course, you know something different." His stare burned a hole right though me.

Right then, I wondered why Abdul-Jalil had never brought back any evidence from Jabal al Lawz. But then, what could he bring back other than photos like I had? And why would a Muslim want to do that? For a fleeting second,

I wondered if I should divulge the photos I took or that the rock he now possessed had been taken from its pinnacle. Instead I moved the subject back to a safe topic—the stones.

"You've only got eleven stones here, one is missing."

"I believe Mort Saul knew where it is," said Misha.

"Why would you think that?" My tone had a defensive edge to it.

"That note I showed you with Mort's name on it was given to me by someone who has led me to several of the stones in the past. The man indicated that Mort was central to finding the stone."

"And this man is reputable?"

"You should know."

My palm slapped my chest. "Me? How should I know?"

"It was Abdul-Jalil."

My head started spinning and I felt as though I was in some sort of time warp, physically in the present but not really there. If what Misha was telling me was true and Mort did know where the stone was, it could be the reason he was killed. Unfortunately, that didn't get me closer to his killer unless I could find the person who knew as much as he did. I certainly wished Misha had told me all this before my clandestine trip with Abdul-Jalil to Jabal al Lawz. I would have had a long conversation with him regarding this connection.

"Why would Abdul-Jalil, an Arab, help you, a Jew, verify that the Exodus took place whether it was twelve stones or Jabal al Lawz? Wouldn't that be counter to his culture and religion?"

"Money makes the world go around."

"Didn't you ask Abdul-Jalil how he knew Mort and why he thinks Mort has the stone?"

"He wouldn't have told me," said Misha.

"Why not?"

"He's never told me how he got the information about the other stones. I knew it was futile to ask him this time. Besides, I don't know how to contact him."

"But you contacted him when you arranged the trip to Jabal al Lawz for me."

"That was done through intermediaries. Now that he took you to the mountain he'll disappear for a while, afraid someone might discover that it was he who took you there. Finding him would be impossible."

"So, you're still looking for the twelfth stone, and I'm still looking for Mort's killer."

"Seems so, and I have no doubt that they are related," said Misha, putting the lids on the boxes.

"Wait!" I said still looking at the stones. "What's this?" I pointed to a light impression in one of the stones that looked like it was deliberately made.

"Hebrew words. When the stones are put together in the correct order, they will make sense—a message from

God. Right now they are just words. I must have that twelfth stone."

I had come all the way to Israel only to discover that Mort knew where the stone was and was probably killed because of it. I needed to get back to South Florida and try to figure out just where Mort might have stashed that twelfth stone.

Chapter 17

Rosa's and my trip back to Florida was uneventful, yet the coolness that permeated the space between us rendered our communications civil but hardly warm. Occasionally, there were hints of forgiveness and our former relationship—a touch here, a look there—but mostly I had become an acquaintance with whom one could have only a surface chat. I didn't know how long this would last, but I swore right then and there that after this mystery was brought to a conclusion I was through with The Consigned and anything else that smelled like trouble. I had pushed Rosa's tolerance to the limit.

Once we returned to Deerfield Beach, I slept in the guest bedroom. I had bedded there upon occasion during my last mysteries, but the length of this episode broke all records. This time I was there so long that the surroundings, decorated for a part time guest, started to feel like home. I missed Rosa's smell with its hint of powder, the feel of her skin, and the warmth of her body snuggling next to mine. I did what I could to extract myself from this painful situation through acts of kindness and vows never to get involved again, but I did feel obligated to finish what I started regarding Mort's death. I trudged along keeping busy with new article assignments and trying to bring this case to a close.

My first stop was Pastor Dan E. Powell's office. I had wanted to go through the book of Exodus myself to try to understand the passages in context with the photos I'd taken on Jabal al Lawz, but I figured Dan could do a far better job of explaining things than my going it alone. Carrying my laptop computer I entered Dan's office at Imperial Point Community Church. Perhaps I could get a little marital counseling while I was there as well.

"Shea, so good to see you." Dan and I embraced like old friends. "How was your trip?"

"Interesting to say the least." I took a seat at the round table in his office.

Dan already had a map stretched out on the table top with his Bible. He looked at me quizzically.

"A little encounter with a door?" He gestured toward my healing black eyes, cuts and still swollen nose.

"No, a rifle," I said.

Dan dropped into his chair, his eyes wide with disbelief. "How in the world?"

I relayed my story about Mort's death, talking to Professor Belenski and being invited on the dig, meeting Misha at the museum, and my subsequent arrangements for my trip to Jabal al Lawz. He sat mesmerized by the tale.

"Shea, did Rosa know about this trip?"

"Not exactly," I said, a trace of hesitation in my voice.

"Sleeping on the couch?"

"The guest room. We're trying to work through it all just now."

"After your relationship with God, your wife needs to be your next priority. I'm sure you know that, but sometimes it takes situations like these for us to be shocked back to reality. Men tend to become locked in their own little world with everyone else just spectators, but that's not how God intended it to be."

"I've certainly got some long fences to mend, and I'm working on it. Just don't know how long I'll be out on the range."

"Well, let's get to the reason why you're here, then we'll pray for your marriage."

I opened my laptop and turned it on. The photos started with our trip from the way station to Jabal al Lawz.

"The sun is just coming up here," I said, showing the sandy trail and the sun light playing among the mountain peaks. "Right here we came upon dozens of palm trees. It was the craziest thing I'd ever seen. All of a sudden, there they were. I'd heard of the desert oasis and I guess this qualifies as one of them."

"Wait a minute," said Dan. He flipped the pages of his bible. "Here it is—Exodus 16: 22-25. Let me set the stage for you. The Israelites have just crossed the Red Sea and are walking through the desert. They are thirsty so they grumble against Moses. Then they came to Mara where there were springs, but the water is bitter. God tells Moses to throw a piece of wood into the spring and the water becomes sweet. Did you see any springs like this?"

"It was still dark when we started toward Jabal al Lawz so I didn't see anything except the road and the palms, of course, illuminated by the headlights. The springs could have been there, but we didn't see them or stop."

"Well, here's the part I wanted to read to you. It's from Exodus 16:27:

Then they came to Elim, where there were twelve springs and seventy palm trees, and they camped there near the water."

"There were dozens of palms. Could that be what we saw—Elim?"

"It's possible," said Dan, "but let's go on. Tell me what you saw when you got to Jabal al Lawz."

169

I showed Dan the photo of the large rocks with the petroglyphs of cows on them. He inspected them carefully, zooming in on the renderings.

"Fascinating," he said.

"Abdul-Jalil indicated that this was the altar where Aaron put the golden calf."

"Let's see what the Bible says." Dan found the passages and read them. The verses were the same as I had remembered—Moses went up to the mountain to talk with God, the people thought he wasn't going to return, they molded a golden calf from their jewelry, set it on an alter and worshiped it. When Moses returned he was angry with the people and broke the clay tablets containing the Ten Commandments.

"What do you think?" I asked.

"It does line up with scripture," Dan said, "but it's certainly not conclusive evidence that the large stones are the altar where the golden calf was placed or that this site is Mt. Sinai."

I advanced to the next set of photos. The images showed the rocks on which were sketched the remarkable outline of feet. Dan looked curiously at them.

"What do you make of these?" he asked.

"I don't really know except I saw a number of flat rocks at the bottom of the mountain, all with these outlines."

"I'm just speculating here, but perhaps these were signs left by the Israelites to fulfill God's promise that wherever they placed their feet would be their land," Dan said.

Next, I showed Dan the photos of my climb up Jabal al Lawz to the summit and the shot of the top of the mountain with its charred surface. The distinct line delineating the burned area from the rest of the mountain could readily be seen. I also told him about breaking the rock and that it was being tested.

"This is getting more interesting all the time," Dan said. "Listen to what the Bible says about Mt. Sinai in Exodus 19:16-19 and 24:17:

> *On the morning of the third day, there was thunder and lightning with a thick cloud over the mountain . . . Mount Sinai was covered with smoke, because the Lord descended on it in fire. The smoke billowed up from it like smoke from a furnace, and the whole mountain trembled violently . . . To the Israelites the glory of the Lord looked like a consuming fire on top of the mountain . . ."*

Dan and I eyeballed each other as goose flesh marched up my arms and neck.

"Could this be why it was black as coal, that it was burned when God descended on it?"

"It certainly lines up with scripture, but until we have the analysis from your rock we won't know for sure just what caused the mountain to turn black," said Dan.

My hands trembled as I arrowed to the next photo I had taken from the top of the mountain looking down at the base.

"What are those?" asked Dan pointing to an obscure discoloration on the photo. His discerning eye had caught something I had never even noticed—several small outcroppings set against the sand. I arrowed forward to a photo I had taken that zoomed in on the area. Piles of rocks could be seen at even intervals around the base of the mountain.

"What do you think they are?"

"I'm not sure," he said, "but they may be markers."

"Markers? Why?"

"In biblical times, herdsmen and farmers didn't have any fences or barbed wire so they marked their property lines with what was readily available—stones. Since God warned the people that they should not approach the mountain or touch it upon penalty of death, these piles of rocks may have been Moses's way of marking the mountain's boundaries." Dan ran his finger down the page and stopped at verse 23. "Here's the reference:

Moses said to the Lord, 'The people cannot come up Mount Sinai, because you yourself warned us, 'Put limits around the mountain and set it apart as holy.'"

To me, the inference was unmistakable—the multiple piles of stones were the property markers that told the Israelites they could come this far but not any farther. The goose bumps were moving faster now, covering my whole body. I arrowed forward.

The next photo was of the v-shaped stone chute and the round sections of columns lying on the ground. Without a word, Powell flipped the pages of the Bible until he came to Exodus 24:4. He slid the Bible toward me and pointed at the verse. It and the next two verses read:

> . . . *He got up early the next morning and built an altar at the foot of the mountain and set up twelve stone pillars representing the twelve tribes of Israel. Then he sent young Israelite men, and they offered burnt offerings and sacrificed young bulls as fellowship offerings to the Lord.*

I was speechless. Apparently, so was the pastor. All we could do was stare at the photo until I arrowed forward to the next one—the monolithic rock. I described its unexpected location on the distant outcropping.

We zoomed in. It was then I realized that the rock wasn't just one monolith but two with a distinct space between them that one couldn't see from a distance. It was obvious by following the contour of the huge rock that it had originally been a single one that had been split right down the middle by some incredible force. Below the monoliths, a river of rocks flowed down an incline and onto the desert floor eventually flattening out in a kind of dry lake bed.

Dan's eyes remained glued to the photo as he examined every aspect of it even arrowing back and forth between distant photos and closer ups.

"Were you able to get closer to the rock?" His eyes never wavered from the screen.

"Unfortunately, no. We were planning to head there when the soldiers caught us. What do you think it is?" I asked.

"I can't say for certain, mind you, but it's possible this could be the rock Moses hewed with his staff to provide water for the Israelites. See here?" He pointed at the rocks flowing down from the monoliths. "This shows evidence of water having eroded their surface and smoothing them out, and this plain of sand is where the run off may have collected into a small lake. The Israelites would have collected water upstream for drinking and allowed their herds to drink from the lake."

Once again, Dan flipped pages from his Bible until he got to Psalms: 78: 15-16:

> *He split the rocks in the wilderness and gave*
> *them water as abundant as the seas; he*

brought streams out of a rocky crag and made water flow down like rivers.

The goose bumps winging across my skin were now so prevalent I felt I had been transformed into one of the flying foul. We sat in silence trying to take in what the amazing photos showed and the corresponding scripture to explain it.

"You know, of course, that these photos are very valuable. Please make copies of them and put them somewhere safe," suggested Dan.

"I will, I assure you," I said. "So what is your best take on what I've shown you?"

Dan sat back and took a deep breath.

"I'm sure you're aware that others dispute Jabal al Lawz as being Mt. Sinai, but then they have yet to declare another mountain the true location. And the truth is, until credentialed scientists and archeologists are allowed to examine the site, we'll never know. Up to this time, it's apparent the Saudis have been unwilling to allow this kind of scrutiny. But I can say with all sincerity that after seeing your photos, if Jabal al Lawz were on trial for being Mt. Sinai, the jury would declare it 'Guilty!' But let's see what Dr. Reuben says about your rock first."

I anxiously waited for Misha to return the rock and the results of the laboratory testing. In the meantime, I still had a murder to solve and a marriage to repair. Before I left,

Dan laid a hand on my shoulder and prayed for Rosa and me.

Upon leaving his office, I knew there was only one way for me to restore my relationship with Rosa—I needed to come clean and tell her the whole story. It was a gamble, of course, but just how worse could it get? I loved Rosa more than anything, and she deserved to know why I went to Jabal al Lawz and what really happened to me, no matter the cost.

That night, I confessed the whole thing—the reason for the trip, what I saw, the photos, the real story about the assault, why my passport was in the gas can, the whole shebang. She vented, but was also amazed I had risked my life for such invaluable information. I begged forgiveness. She cried. I cried.

Confession is good for the soul; I was living proof. That night I felt like a new man sleeping in my own bed with Rosa beside me. Of course, we still had things to work through, but I was optimistic I could stick to the narrow path even while working to solve Mort's murder and unravel the mystery of the twelfth stone. And then, of course, there was still the issue of the temple member's being all too anxious to be buried in the mausoleum. I didn't have a clue how that was to unravel, but somehow I felt more than ever that these untimely deaths, Mort's murder, the twelfth stone and even Jabal al Lawz were somehow entwined.

Chapter 18

I phoned Detective Warren the next morning to check in and see if there was any news on Mort's killer. He wasn't in; I left a message. I also phoned Stella to let her know I was back and to see if she had any more information regarding the temple deaths. She wasn't in either. Another message. Next on my list was Helen Lechner. Thankfully, she was in.

"Shea, so nice to hear from you. Did you have a nice trip?"

I wasn't sure how to answer her.

"Yes and no," I finally said.

"Well, that sounds a bit noncommittal," said Helen. "Do you want to talk about it?"

I hesitated a moment tossing around the idea that another woman could throw some perspective on the situation. In the end, however, I decided against it.

"Another time perhaps, right now I want to see how you are and if there is any more news."

"Well, I'm fine, but I can't say the same for Cynthia Kornblath."

"Another death?"

"Yes, and she was only sixty-eight."

"What was her cause of death?"

"They say a heart attack. But Cynthia was strong. Played golf. Went to the gym. Never sick a day in her life. Then all of a sudden, blam! Keels over right in her living room. They didn't find her until several days later, her being a widow and living by herself. It reminded me too much of what happened to Gertrude Ginsberg. She was inurned a couple of months ago."

Stella had already emailed me the information she had amassed regarding the temple burials cross referenced by post mortem purchases. I pulled out my list and checked the names. Sure enough, Gertrude Ginsberg was on the list. She had died of a heart attack before all this mystery with Mort, and her family had purchased her niche *after* her death. Cynthia Kornblath had died while I was gone and was interred in the mausoleum. Like Gertrude, her space had been purchased by the family *after* her death.

"So you think her death is part of the conspiracy?" I had never put a name to the uncanny series of deaths and burials, but it seemed to fit.

"Yes, and who knows who's next." Helen's voice radiated trepidation.

"Look, Helen, if you're that concerned, it's time to bring in the police."

"With all due respect," she said softly, resignation in her voice, "they've got more important things to do then to go off on some wild goose chase started by an old woman who *thinks* something's fishy. Even with what you have, we need more evidence. What we need is—" Her voice trailed off into oblivion, incapable of volume. Then, as if she had found some sort of mysterious energy, she finished her sentence, "—a sting operation."

"A sting operation?" I could hardly believe my ears.

"Sure. You know, a set up," she said nonchalantly, as though she conducted these things all the time. "We get a couple to join the Temple. They get an appointment with the salesperson at the mausoleum. They seem interested but not committed. Then we let things run their course." Her tone of apprehension had vanished, replaced by enthusiastic determination. I could envision her devious grin as she spoke.

"So, you want someone to put their life in jeopardy?"

"Look, Shea, lots of lives are in jeopardy the longer this goes on. Don't you think my idea is worth a try?"

I had just gotten out of the dog house; I certainly didn't want to crawl back in.

"No. No I don't," I said with conviction. "And don't you go setting this up yourself. It's too dangerous. There may be another way, one we haven't thought of yet. Give me a day or two and I'll get back to you."

"Sting operation," she repeated. "It's the only way."

Upon hanging up, my computer serenaded me; I had an email. It was from Dr. Reuben. My heart leapt to my throat and I took a deep breath as I clicked it open.

Dear Shea,

I've attached the lab results on your rock and I've taken the liberty to interpret what it says in layman's terms. I hope it's what you expected.

While I realize I told you I'd send the rock back, I've decided to keep it, at least for a little while, until we discover the whereabouts of the twelfth stone. That should give you some incentive to plough ahead.

Best regards to you and Rosa.

Misha

I had a few choice words for the ancient double crossing relic digger, but I settled on giving him a single demerit for his failed promise. After all, we're supposed to forgive. Besides, he did keep some of his word—testing the rock and sending me the results.

Opening the attachment, the first page contained a diagram indicating the composition of the rock and the percentage of each type of mineral it contained. These figures meant nada to me. I didn't know one mineral from another and had no clue what all the text and figures meant, but Misha's explanation, a mini geology lesson, was of great interest:

> *There are three types of rocks: igneous, sedimentary, and metamorphic.*
>
> *Igneous rocks - crystalline solids that form directly from the cooling of magma - molten rock (called lava when it reaches the earth's surface). This is an exothermic process meaning that the cooling process involves a stage change from the liquid to the solid state. The earth's crust is made up of igneous rocks. (examples: granite, pumice, obsidian, etc.)*
>
> *Sedimentary rocks – also called secondary, because they are often the result of the accumulation of small pieces broken off of pre-existing rocks. The rock is made up of layers of this debris that become*

compacted and cemented together and account for the thin layer that covers the earth's surface. (examples: limestone, shale, sandstone, etc.)

Metamorphic rocks - the name comes from "meta" (change) and "morph" (form). Any rock can become a metamorphic rock. All that is required is for the rock to be exposed to an environment in which the minerals in the rock become unstable and out of equilibrium with the new environmental conditions. This typically occurs by a rise in temperature and pressure. (examples: slate, marble, quartzite, etc.)

Sample A (your rock) – The majority of your rock is igneous. However, the lab took a thin slice of the top portion of the rock (the black portion) and reported it to be a metamorphic rock. The scientists who examined the rock have no explanation as to how this occurred.

The lab's findings were significant. While the majority of the mountain had remained the same since its formation, the top had undergone some sort of transformation. If I was a betting man, I'd go all in that profound heat had caused the stone to turn black rather than pressure. Could the Bible's explanation—that God had descended upon it in fire—have been the catalyst for this change? I phoned Dr. Powell and told him of the lab's findings. He agreed that the report was just one more piece of evidence that, along with the photos and the Bible's account of the Israelites encampment, could render a "guilty" verdict for Jabal al Lawz being Mt. Sinai.

Now that I knew about the rock, the rest of the Israelite's trek from Mt. Sinai to crossing the Jordan River and the establishment of the twelve stones as a memorial had more evidence to back them up. The problem was, however, that since no prominent scientists or archeologists had been to Jabal al Lawz to validate or dispute what I had seen, proof of the Exodus and the Israelites crossing the Jordan River still fell squarely on the revelation of Misha's twelve stones.

As I was pondering this heavy weight, Detective Warren phoned.

"Hi, Baker, have a nice trip?"

"I guess you could say that."

"You sound a bit hesitant. Anything you want to talk about?"

First Helen, and now Warren. Did I sound like I needed a confessor?

"Not really," I responded.

"How's the nose? Healing properly I hope."

"How'd you know about that?"

"Don't know why you even ask that question. Like I told you before, I know everything."

He was right. I don't know why I asked that question. He, Sheriff Berry before him, and The Consigned seemed to know my every move. I wondered if they were all in cahoots, perhaps even listening in on my cell phone calls. Or had they somehow mysteriously implanted a tracking device under my skin? I looked at my forearms for any recent incisions.

"Any further news on Mort's killer?" I asked.

"Maybe I should be asking *you* that question."

"Me? Why would you say that?"

"Aren't you the one that just got back from Israel, from meeting with Dr. Reuben, from taking a little side trip to Jabal al Lawz? By the way, how did that journey help in your quest for answers about Mort's killer?"

Now I was certain they were all in it together. Otherwise, how was he able to find out all about my "little side trip?" Someone, The Consigned, I was convinced, had saved me in the desert and had communicated such to Berry's office. While they knew about Dr. Reuben, it was obvious they didn't know how the twelfth stone and Reuben were tied together or that Mort was involved.

"The side trip was just a whim. Trying to understand the scriptural version of the Exodus," I said.

"Didn't know you were such a scholar of scripture."

"Ah ha," I said with enthusiastic conviction. "Your bullet proof vest has been pierced. You just admitted that you don't know everything."

Quiet prevailed; a smug smirk etched my lips.

"Well, keep in touch. We're still very interested in any information that will help further the investigation. And Baker?"

"What?"

"Keep your nose straight and out of trouble." I could hear Warren chuckling as he hung up the phone.

I found Rosa in the kitchen putting together a late breakfast of fruit and yogurt. I wrapped my arms around her waist, held her tight, and planted several kisses on the back of her neck. I then moved to her ear.

"Thank you," I whispered with all sincerity, glad to be back in the relationship. She turned around.

"You're welcome," she responded with a kiss. "Just don't let it happen again." Her stern brown and piercing eyes spoke volumes. "Oh, I meant to tell you, Mary Anne called. She said Meyer had to cut his summer dig short and they're back in Boca. They've asked us to dinner tonight. I told her 'yes.' We're invited for seven."

I kissed Rosa's cheek softly, my version of 'ok,' then went back to my office for more musing about the twelfth stone. I clicked open the folder on my computer that contained the photos I took at the Mausoleum after Mort's funeral. I thought if I perused each one carefully I might find something useful. Thirty minutes into my search, two photos jumped out at me. The first one was of the back of the mystery man that took off when he saw me. I didn't recognize him, though something about him looked familiar. Maybe Helen would know who he was. I printed out what images I had and made a note to call the diminutive woman and make a date.

The next photo was of the Rosenblum Chapel. Bordered by walls of crypts, its long corridor, inlaid with the Star of David, ran down the length of the chapel to a back wall of niches. It was there about waist high that I saw something I hadn't noticed before. One of the niches appeared to have a reflective front to it instead of a marble front like all the others. In fact, it looked like it had a glass window one could peer through. Beyond the glass and inside the niche, there appeared to be some sort of dark object. I zoomed in for a closer look. It looked eerily similar in size, shape and color to the eleven stones in Misha Reuben's vault. I enlarged it further. Unfortunately, the image became so pixilated that it was impossible to determine any specifics. As I toggled back and forth between normal and close up photos, my journalistic sixth sense surged through me like a jolt of electricity. I instinctively knew that I had to go down to the Mausoleum right then and see for myself what was inside the glass enclosed niche. I grabbed my old back up camera, the printed photo, kissed Rosa goodbye and was off.

Cars lined the access road as I pulled into the cemetery, and next door at the temple, there didn't seem to be one empty parking space. By the looks of things and because it was the middle of the week, I figured someone big in the community had died. Sure enough, just as I found a parking space at the end of the exit route, hordes poured from the temple doors heading for the mausoleum. If I jogged, I'd have just enough time to arrive before they did, take a look at the niche in question and perhaps take a few photos. I grabbed my equipment and placed my Sunshine Media press pass around my neck. I kept it in the car for 'just in case' times.

I was about to break into my trot when a man approached dressed in a black suit. I surmised he was an attendant with the funeral home.

"Sorry, sir, but you can't park there. Didn't you see the 'No Parking' sign?" He pointed to a small square metal sign flattened on the ground in front of my vehicle.

"Sorry, but I didn't."

He looked at me then back at the sign. It was clear he was inferring that I had laid the sign low. "Well, regardless," he said, "you'll have to find another spot."

Glancing over the suit's shoulder, I could see the mourners closing the distance to the mausoleum as they undulated their way through the parking lot.

"Look," I countered in my friendliest voice, "I'm sorry about the sign but I'm really late. My editor will have my tush if I don't get this photo. Can't you overlook this?" I flashed him my friendliest grin and press pass.

"You already missed Mr. Shapiro's funeral."

"I know that's why I need to get this shot." I glanced again over the man's shoulder to see the mourners more than half way to the mausoleum. I needed to move quickly. To help motivate the man, I pulled a fifty dollar bill from my money clip. "Please?" I pleaded, waving the bill in front of me.

Black suit looked around cautiously, then snatched the fifty and stepped aside. I high tailed it to the building, but this out of shape Baby Boomer wasn't quick enough. Just as I arrived so did the throng of mourners. Panting, I stood back and discretely took a number of photos as the crowd entered the three-story air conditioned mausoleum. Fifteen minutes later the ceremony was over and the mourners dispersed. Less than a handful milled around as the others headed towards their cars or back to the temple.

"Such a shame," said a dark haired woman to her male companion as they walked past me. "And so young. He was only 50. I'm sure Abe is devastated to know that Craig died in such a tragic way." The woman shook her head from side to side.

I knew the name Abe Shapiro. He was one of Boca Raton's premier commercial real estate owners, and he ran a string of realty offices. The couple must have been talking about his son Craig, heir to the considerable empire.

"To actually die by plunging into a canal and drowning," said the man, his head down. "What an awful way to go. But then, it happens all the time down here."

My ears perked up at the cause of death and the man's young age. Could this be another death in Helen's so called "conspiracy?" I took a photo of the couple as they got into their Mercedes. When I talked with Helen, I'd see if she knew anything about it.

As the bereaved departed, I made my way down the Chapel toward the glass fronted niche. I thought I'd be able to see what was inside from a distance but light coming from the rotunda reflected off the glass rendering it impossible unless you were right in front of it. When I arrived at the niche, I bent down and peered inside with great anticipation. My heart lurched to a stop at what I saw.

Chapter 19

I ran back to my car, jumped in and headed down Camino Real toward A1A. The posted speed limit wasn't high enough to get me to Helen's as fast as I hoped, so I phoned to let her know I was coming. She immediately ushered me into her condo. This time we sat in her living room.

"What's so important, Shea? I hope you've come to tell me you've found a way to catch the killer." She sat on the edge of her chair and looked at me wide eyed.

"Perhaps," I said, "but first I need to ask you a few questions. Do you recognize this man?" I pulled out the printed photo of the mystery man I took after Mort's funeral. She looked carefully at it.

"He looks familiar, but I'm not quite certain."

"What about these folks?" I showed her the digital image on my camera of the couple I had just photographed at Abe Shapiro's funeral.

"Oh yes, this couple is Ruth and Ron Welsh. He's president of First Union bank." Helen sat back and brought her hand to her chest. "Do you think they're involved with the murders?"

"No, of course not," I said, patting Helen's knee in reassurance, "but they were just at the funeral for Abe Shapiro's son, Craig. I heard them talking about how young he was and how he died."

"Yes, such a tragedy. I read about it. Are you thinking Craig was one of our victims?"

"Honestly, I don't know, but I'll have Stella cross reference his name with our list. Here, take a look at these other photos and see if you recognize anyone." I showed Helen the digital photos on my camera. She was able to name a number of temple members.

"Wait, go back," said Helen. She pointed her thin frail index finger at a photo. "Isn't that the man in the printed photo you showed me? The one who was at Mort's funeral?" She picked up the printed photo and held it next to the digital photo that I had enlarged. We both looked intently from one image to the other.

"They do look similar," I said.

"Similar!" she gasped. "Why he's wearing the same clothes. He's got to be the same man. Maybe he attended the other funerals as well."

I remembered that Detective Warren had attended Mort's funeral to see if the perpetrator had returned to the scene of the crime.

"Now, Helen," I said, squaring myself and looking directly into her eyes, "what I'm about to ask you is very important.

"Okay," she said. Her hazel eyes searched mine.

"The glass enclosed niche in the Rosenblum Chapel, what do you know about it?"

"Oh, that. It was Mort's idea," she said with a wave of her hand. "He had taken so many trips to Israel that he wanted to bring back something that would remind us of our Jewish roots."

"Do you know what that 'something' was?

"Sure. It was a stone, and a pretty big one at that."

"Do you know where he got it?"

"Not really, other than he said it had come from Beth Shalom, a village close to the Jordan River. The temple was named after the village."

"Did you ever see the rock before it was installed in the niche?"

Helen looked at me quizzically. "What's this all about, Shea?"

"I can't say just now, but it may have something to do with Mort's murder."

Helen gasped. "Are you saying the stone from Beth Shalom may have killed Mort? I thought someone hit him with a brass vase?"

"I'm not talking about the weapon used in his death."

Helen looked deep in thought. "Then you're talking about motive." Her forehead creased, and she looked at me with unyielding eyes.

I was silent. I knew Helen was a smart cookie but didn't think she'd figure this out. She moved to the edge of her seat waiting for further explanation.

"It's complicated," I said, my hand caressing my thinning hair. "Right now there are two possible motives and I don't know which one is right. Because of that, I need your help."

"Whatever you need," she said.

"I came right here from the Shapiro funeral, but I wasn't there to honor the memory of Abe's son Craig. I didn't even know the man. I was there to see what was in the niche. When I looked through the glass, I was stunned. It's empty."

"Yes, I know," said Helen in a nonchalant manner. "Someone broke the glass and stole the stone. The temple reported it to the police and replaced the glass, but we're still wondering why someone would want that old thing. I mean, it sat there for fifteen years then all of a sudden it disappeared. Now you're telling me it may be the motive for Mort's death. If it was, the break-in and the stone's disappearance would make much more sense. How can I help?"

"First, I need you to keep what I've just told you to yourself. Second, I need a photograph of the stone. Surely one exists. A copy was probably given to the police when the theft was reported."

"Let me check with the temple. I'll need a reason for asking." Helen brought her finger tips to her temples and closed her eyes. I could sense a whirling mind behind her hazel eyes. "I know," she said, her eyes popping open. "As a member of the committee, I'll volunteer to look into replacing the stone with another one from Beth Shalom. But I'll want to replace it with a close look alike. Leave it to me, Shea, I'll get you a photo." She jabbed her index finger into the air for emphasis.

I bid Helen goodbye and we vowed to check in with each other tomorrow.

Heading home, I phoned Stella. I hadn't talked to her in a few days and now I needed her to locate some important information for me.

"Hi pardner," I said into my hands free mobile device in my best rendition of The Duke. Stella laughed.

"Hi, yourself, Boss. How are things going? Found the killer yet?" She seemed her usual perky self.

"Not, yet, but we're getting closer. I need you to do a little research."

"Lay it on me."

If I knew Stella, she had grabbed her notebook computer and would be typing away as I gave her instructions.

"Check out a man named Craig Shapiro, son of Abe Shapiro, the Boca real estate mogul. Find out the when, where, and how of his death. You know, the usual info we've been looking into. Also, whether his crypt was purchased before or after his death."

"Anything else?"

"Yes. See if you can find any newspaper articles when the mausoleum was dedicated. What I'm looking for is something about a stone from Israel that was installed in a niche in the Rosenberg Chapel. Don't bother with my article, I didn't write about the topic I'm interested in, but the papers might have. Also, try to locate the reporters who wrote the story. I'd like to speak with them personally."

"A stone?"

"Yes. I'm specifically looking for a photo of it. If you find one, get in touch with the media that ran the story and purchase an original or digital copy. Oh, and see if they have any additional photos. They always take scores of photos at dedications, but I'm not sure they'd keep all of them. It's a long shot, but ask anyway." I wanted a backup plan in case Helen couldn't locate the photo through the mausoleum committee.

"How soon do you need the info?"

"Yesterday," I said. I figured Stella's computer expertise and geek abilities would be able to acquire this information at lightning speed.

"I should have seen that coming. I'll get right on it. Oh, wait . . . I have a date tonight. Can it wait until tomorrow?"

"A date? Why Stella, I've never heard you mention a date before. I hope it's someone special."

"We'll see. I'll call you tomorrow."

When I got home, Rosa was in the laundry room folding clothes. I planted a kiss on her cheek then turned toward my office.

"Don't forget about our date tonight with the Belinskys. We need to be there at seven," she called over her shoulder after me.

Back in my office, I sat down at the computer and stared blankly at the screen hoping for some revelation that would unravel this new mystery—the whereabouts of the Beth Shalom stone, who took it, and whether it was, in fact, the twelfth stone. The theft would only make sense if, as I supposed, the thief knew its significance.

It had already been both an enlightening and confusing day. By the night's end, it was to become even more so.

The Belinskys lived in Boca West, a fourteen hundred acre upscale development in an unincorporated area west of the city and just off the busiest road in the area— Glades Road. The road ran east to west, from US1 in the city to the Everglades. Back in the early 1900s, the then narrow sandy road was bordered by bean fields, the main staple of the growing agricultural community. Today, that area was covered by residential developments and country clubs. The multiple villages of Boca West consisted of condos, town homes, villas and single-family homes surrounded by four golf courses, canals and small lakes. I'd been there dozens of times interviewing top executives as well as covering elite events. The Belinskys lived in a patio home that overlooked the third fairway of The Hibiscus, the second golf course.

Mary Ann greeted both Rosa and me with a broad smile and air kisses. "You look no worse for wear," she said, inspecting my nose. "I do hope you're well healed."

"As good as it's going to get," I said. Meyer and I shook hands.

Rosa and Mary Anne linked arms and didn't skip a conversational beat as they walked to the dining room. I was a bit more cautious with Meyer. He didn't know that I knew he had threatened Misha, and I wanted to keep it that way, but there were several questions I wanted answers to. Perhaps I could get to them during the course of the evening.

Dinner consisted of shrimp scampi served with a large helping of chit chat. After dinner, Meyer served drinks on their screened in lanai. The overhead fans cooled us in the evening's waning warm temperatures and shadows from coconut palms bordering the golf course fairway grew long. While Rosa and Mary Anne chatted away like magpies, Meyer and I fell into our own conversation.

"Rosa tells me you had to cut your summer dig short. I hope it was nothing too serious that brought you back to Florida."

"Serious enough, but it has all worked out. What about you? While you were in Jerusalem were you able to find answers to your questions regarding the twelfth stone?"

I shot Meyer a quizzical look.

"So sorry," he said. "What I meant was, were you able to find out more about the twelve stones?" He looked at me over the rim of his glass as he took a sip of his liqueur. I wasn't sure whether he knew about the twelfth stone and I should play along, or drop the whole conversation. I decided to play along.

"Well, I got diverse answers from a number of different people, but they all seemed to agree . . . the stones have great importance to the history of the Jewish people. The hope is that someday the stones will resurface to confirm once and for all that the Exodus really did occur. Wouldn't that be something if the twelve stones were actually found?"

Meyer hesitated a moment, then let out a hearty laugh. "It's purely wishful thinking. As I told you, no evidence exists today or will exist in the future to substantiate the Exodus. It simply never occurred. There are no twelve stones."

I moved to the edge of my seat and looked Meyer straight in the eye. I was about to stick a dagger deep into his persona. "But what if there were?"

Meyer appeared dumbstruck. "Look, Shea," he said, speaking in an exasperated tone, as though I were a child that needed to have the explanation repeated, "I've spent my whole academic life researching, reporting and writing on the nonexistence of the Exodus. I'm not about to speculate on some nonsense that it did occur. There's just no evidence."

I twisted the blade.

"But, what if there *was* evidence? What if by some miracle the stones were found."

"No one will ever find them. They simply don't exist." Meyer's words and tone were controlled, but his taught trembling lips, crinkled brow and stern eyes said my blade was hitting its mark.

I twisted the dagger in deeper.

"But, what if they did? What, if by some hypothetical circumstance, one of the stones wound up right here in South Florida?"

Meyer jumped from his chair.

"Ridiculous! Ridiculous!" he yelled in an animated tone. "You've offered nothing but speculation. The stones don't exist I tell you. They don't exist!"

"What's going on over there?" asked Mary Anne who had turned from her conversation with Rosa to see her red-faced flustered husband.

That was my cue.

"Bathroom?" I asked.

"Down the hall, across from Meyer's study," said Mary Anne.

I excused myself and made my way down the hall, a broad smirk on my lips. I had touched a raw nerve. I didn't quite know how it fit into the equation, but I knew it did somehow.

Opposite the bathroom, the door to Meyer's study was ajar. I peeked in. A dim light from a standing lamp illuminated a desk as cluttered as the one at his university office—open books, papers, a camera, empty glass—all lying on the top in disarray. Behind his desk, a multitude of artifacts were displayed on three long crowded bookshelves. I scanned the hall furtively. Seeing no one and still hearing Mary Anne trying to calm her husband, I opened the door and stepped in.

The artifacts—shards of pottery, clay necklaces, statuary, glass beads, small carvings—sat crammed together on the shelves. A thin layer of dust covered the items as well as the shelves except for one area in the corner on the bottom shelf. There, a tall pitcher had been moved to accommodate something behind it. Being the curious sort that I am, I bent in to get a closer look. Though the faint glow from the lamp wasn't enough to discern details, there was no mistaking what it was—a large stone.

I withdrew my phone and used my flashlight app to illuminate the object. It appeared to be the same size, shape, and color as the ones in Misha Reuben's cabinet. It was then a flashlight app of my own switched on inside my head. Was this the stone that was stolen from the mausoleum? Was this the twelfth stone?

I looked for an inscription but couldn't discern any on the part of the stone that I could see. Of course, half the stone was still obscured in shadows in the corner of the bookshelf. Could I risk moving it to take a look? Just as this thought resonated in my brain, I heard someone coming. I took a quick photo of the stone, then slipped out the door and ducked into the bathroom across the hall. Once inside, I immediately flushed the toilet to give whoever might be out there the idea that the bathroom was still occupied. As I did, I heard the distinct sound of the study door close. I ran water in the sink, and washed my hands. As I opened the door to leave, Meyer was standing opposite me in the hall.

"Everything okay?" he asked.

"Took longer than I thought," I said with a smile.

"After you," said Meyer, gesturing that I lead the way back to the lanai.

After a few promises to get together again sometime, we bid the Belinsky's goodbye and drove home. I needed to process what I'd seen and compare my photo with the ones Helen and Stella would hopefully locate through the Mausoleum Committee and newspapers. If they matched, I'd know beyond a shadow of a doubt that Meyer had broken into the niche and stolen the stone. But a big question remained: If this was the stone from the mausoleum and it was Mort's twelfth stone, how did Professor Belinsky find out it was there?

Chapter 20

About ten the next morning, I placed a call to Stella. I figured by then she had enough time to recover from her date and do a little research. I was wrong. She had done neither and said she'd call me back around two. I then put in a call to Helen to see if she had any luck with the photo from the mausoleum. I hit the jackpot.

"Want to take a ride down by the beach?" I asked Rosa. "I have to go pick up something and I want you to meet someone."

"Sure," she said. "It looks like a lovely day and I'm game for getting out of the house. Besides, that cute little restaurant on Palmetto Park Road called the Muffin Tin is calling our names. Maybe your friend would like to join us?"

"Great idea. I'll ask her when we see her."

I'd never involved Rosa directly in my mysteries before, but now I needed her help. I knew she'd initially resist when I broached the subject with her, but getting her to know some of the folks involved would, I believed, help cement my case. We made our way up to Helen's condo where she warmly greeted us.

"Hi Shea. And this must be your beloved wife, Rosa. Please, my dear, come this way." Helen ushered us into her spacious living room.

"Thanks for seeing us on such short notice," I said.

"Shea, you're always welcome. And Rosa, you must be so proud of how your husband goes out of his way to help people, especially little old ladies like myself." Her broad smile was as bright as her artwork.

"Oh, yes. It truly amazes me," said Rosa, shooting me a 'you've got to be kidding me' look.

"I met Helen at Mort's funeral. She was a friend of his and served with him on the temple's mausoleum committee."

Rosa laid a sympathetic hand on Helen's. "His death must have been tragic news to you. I'm so sorry."

"Thank you. Mort was a very special person. Aside from serving on the mausoleum committee with me, he helped me get through my husband's death several years ago. Took me out to dinner on occasion and called every week. He never let me feel alone."

"He obviously was a very thoughtful man," said Rosa. "By the way, Helen, Shea and I are headed to the Muffin Tin for lunch. We'd love for you to join us."

"How very kind, my dear. I'll just grab my sweater. It's always so cold in restaurants and theaters." Helen rose and returned with a black sweater draped around her neck and a manila envelope. "The pictures," she said, holding up the envelope.

Rosa looked quizzically at me. *"Later,"* I mouthed to her.

At the small quaint restaurant, we had a delightful lunch, after which, Helen brought out the photos.

"I believe these are what you wanted." She handed me the envelope.

I rubbed my hands together like an adolescent being handed the keys to his first car. Sorting through the photos—different angles of the stone—I viewed them with great scrutiny then passed them on to Rosa. She briefly scanned them but knew nothing of their significance.

"Do they help?" asked Helen.

"Yes, and no," I said. "They look similar to the ones I saw in Misha's cabinet in the museum, only none of these photos show any kind of inscription. But I'll reserve judgement until I see if Stella turns up anything."

Unexpectedly, Helen let out sob. She grabbed her napkin and dabbed at her eyes. Rosa and I both looked at her with alarm.

"What is it?" asked Rosa, placing a concerned hand on Helen's shoulder.

"It's just that I was hoping the photos would help . . . be the key to finding Mort's killer and perhaps help lead to identifying why the other temple members were murdered too." Helen's eyes brimmed over with tears.

Rosa's eyebrows shot up. "What's this about other members being murdered?"

"There have been a number of temple members buried lately. Helen believes they were murdered, just like Mort," I said.

"That's terrible." Rosa eyes searched mine for comfort.

"Yes, it is. We're trying to figure all this out. We believe the stone stolen from the mausoleum might be key to not only solving Mort's murder but the others too. That's why getting our hands on the stone is so important."

"Well, I'm sure it will surface, and everything will be fine," Rosa said, patting Helen's hand.

We took Helen back to her penthouse then returned home.

"Why didn't you tell me about the possible murders of Helen's temple friends?"

"You know I try to protect you as much as possible. The more you know, the more you're at risk."

"So why tell me now? Why have me meet Helen and hear her sad story?"

"I wanted you two to meet because I need your help?" I tried not to sound too guilty for having orchestrated the meeting and having Helen share her moving story to help Rosa buy into assisting me.

"My help? What could I possibly do to help you find Mort's killer?"

Just as I was about to answer her, my cell rang.

"Boss, I've got the info you wanted. How about Java Joe's in an hour?" said Stella.

"Perfect. See you there."

"Well?" said Rosa expectantly.

"Gotta run. I'll answer your question as soon as I get back from meeting Stella. Your help may just prove to be pivotal in solving Mort's and the other murders." I kissed Rosa on the cheek and made a quick exit.

***

Dressed in black pants, white sleeveless T-shirt and over blouse, Stella had one of her unexpected conservative days. It was nice, but I missed the surprise and excitement of her colorful wardrobe. Her vibrant makeup, however, made up for her two-toned clothes.

"Hi Boss. Does that quirky look on your face mean you like today's look?"

Her eye shadow was a combination of pink and purple, accented by heavy blue mascara and black eyeliner.

Rose-colored blush and dark pink lipstick completed the vivid color pallet.

"It's different and certainly stands out."

"Oh, Boss, you say the nicest things." She gave me a broad smile.

We each ordered coffee and a poppy seed muffin and sat at a table for two near the window. Stella withdrew some papers from her large tote and placed them on the table.

"Before you begin, I'd like to know how the date was?" I raised my eyebrows multiple times in gleeful anticipation of her answer. She merely looked at me with dreamy glassy eyes. Her expression spoke louder than any words she could have voiced. "Okay then," I continued, "Let's see what you have for me."

"We'll start with what I turned up on Craig Shapiro. Aside from what you know—son of real estate mogul Abe Shapiro, VP of his father's company, divorced, age fifty, father of two, man about town—he died, as reported, when his Porsche plunged into the Boca Rio Canal about 3 a.m. on a rainy Sunday morning. According to the autopsy, the alcohol level in his blood was .08, just at the legal limit, and the police investigation on the car reported scrapes and dents on the rear bumper. His father stated that his son had been involved in a fender bender the week before, though no police report was filed. The police attributed the bumper scrapes to that altercation, so no further investigation was made. The coroner stated his death as an accident with alcohol being a contributing factor. His crypt in the mausoleum was purchased after he died. Does that help?"

"Yes and no." As I said those words, it struck me that those two little words seemed to sum up the history of this mystery. "With what we've turned up, as far as I'm concerned he falls onto our list of suspect deaths. How many does that make now?"

Stella brought out her notebook, powered up, and clicked a few keys. "Ten over the past nine months that meet our criteria."

"That's about one a month!" I was amazed at the number. "What else do you have?"

"Nothing more on the mausoleum deaths but here are the articles I found on the mausoleum." Stella pushed a stapled stack of papers toward me. "On top are the names and contact information of the reporters. Beneath the articles are the photos from the newspapers."

I glanced at the articles and reporter's names. Like my article, they didn't seem to mention the stone in the glass niche, but what I really wanted to see were the photos. There was only one that was taken of the glass encasement and it was shot at quite a distance.

"No close ups?" I asked.

"No, but I did have my Photoshop friends blow this one up and focus in on the niche. Here's the photo." She handed me an eight by ten inch glossy. I could have kissed her for thinking ahead.

"The stone appears to be identical to the one in the photo Helen gave me, so from that perspective we know the stone was installed when Mort had the mausoleum built, but I don't see an inscription on any of the stones."

I pulled out the photos Helen gave me and handed them to Stella. She compared them with the ones she had obtained. I also showed her a printout of the photo I took of the glass niche after Mort's funeral.

"You're right, the stones all look the same, so at least you know the stone was still there at Mort's funeral."

"Yes, but someone recently stole it."

"Why would anyone want an old stone, unless—" Her voice trailed off, then the look of revelation appeared in her eyes.

"Exactly. Whoever took the stone knew it was the twelfth one."

"So what's your next move?"

"I'm not sure."

Stella's cell phone sang a tune. She picked it up and looked at the display.

"Well, Boss, if I can help you any more, you know where I am." Stella wrapped up her muffin, put it in her bag and got up to leave.

"Why the hurry?" I asked.

She shot me one of her dreamy glassy-eyed looks.

"Oh, I see. The mystery man. So when do I meet him?"

"Sometime," she said, a grin on her face as she left.

I sat there finishing my coffee and flipping through the photos again. Despite the many images and the fact that the stones looked alike, I still wasn't one hundred percent certain that the stone was actually the twelfth stone. I did, however, have a plan to find out.

Chapter 21

"You want me to what?" Rosa stood in the kitchen, hands on hips and stared at me in shock and disbelief.

"Look, I know it's asking a lot of you, but it's the only way we can be sure it's the twelfth stone."

"But Mary Anne is my friend. What will she think knowing I was involved with such a devious scheme?"

"Mary Anne may be your friend, but believe me, Meyer is not. If he stole that stone and it is what I think it is, he's not only a thief, he's deprived the Jewish people of their heritage and the world of a historic artifact."

I could see Rosa mulling my words over in her mind.

"But I'm not a thief, Shea. I've never stolen anything in my life or been involved in anything like this. And I've certainly never been in trouble with the law. Not even a traffic ticket."

"Believe me, nothing will happen. Do you think Meyer would report a stone stolen from his home when he's the one who stole it from the mausoleum in the first place? No way. He'll be furious, sure, and he'll probably suspect it was us, but he'd never voice it. And I guarantee that he'd never tell Mary Anne. The two of you can still remain friends."

"How could I look Mary Anne in the eye again? Why don't you just get Detective Warren involved? Let him obtain the stone lawfully."

I raked my hand through my hair and paced the room in frustration.

"Right now, there's no evidence that Meyer was even involved with the break in, so I'd have a hard time trying to convince your friend Stan that Meyer stole the stone. Here, look at this?" I withdrew my cell phone, tapped it a few times, and placed it in front of Rosa. "This is the photo I took of the stone Meyer has on his bookshelf." I zoomed in so she could have a closer look.

"How'd you get that?" asked Rosa in utter surprise.

"The night we had dinner at the Belinsky's. But that's not what's important. Look at these and compare them to Belinsky's stone." I showed Rosa the images both

Stella and Helen had given me. "These are the photos from the mausoleum when the dedication took place, and here is a close up of the stone that I took at Mort's funeral." I placed the images and my cell phone side by side on the glass top bistro table in our kitchen.

Rosa looked intently from one image to another. "They do look like the same stone. But how do you know it's the twelfth stone?"

"I don't. The twelfth stone should have an inscription on it, but until we get our hands on Meyer's stone we won't know for sure."

Rosa looked at me, then back to the photos. "I don't know, Shea. I don't think I'm the right woman for this job."

I placed my hands on her shoulders and looked her straight in the eye.

"Look, I've always tried to protect you by keeping you out of situations like this, but now we have no choice. You're not merely the *right* woman for this job; you are the *only* woman for this job. And rest assured that I would never ask you to do such a thing if I didn't think it was of the utmost importance.

"Think of your friend Misha Ruben, what he's gone through for thirty-five years. All the time and effort he's put into trying to find these stones. His dream could become reality, and you could be part of it. Think of the history of the Jewish people, and how this one ancient artifact could bring hope and light to them. Think of Helen, and how getting our hands on this stone could be the key to finding Mort's killer and perhaps uncover the reason why her friends and others have been murdered. Think of how, this one stone could prove to skeptics like Meyer Belinsky and to the world that the Exodus really did take place and the Bible story is true. Think of how you could be involved in one of the most important discoveries of our lifetime, something big, something world altering."

I looked at Rosa with great expectation after delivering such a splendid speech that gave her myriad reasons to say "yes." She, however, simply stood there in deep contemplation.

"But, Shea," she finally said, "you're rationalizing why I should do something that goes against everything I stand for. Does the end always justify the means? Do two wrongs make a right? How do I defend my actions—being adamant against something, then turning around and doing it?" Tears began to fill her eyes.

I released Rosa and stood back. She was right. She had set a line of principles for herself that she would never step over, and I had asked her to do just that—to *be* something she was not, a thief, and *do* something that was against her values, steal—all because I wanted the stone, even if it was for all the right reasons. My motive was altruistic, but my method, suspect. I went to Rosa and drew her to me, wrapping my arms about her and holding her close.

"I'm sorry," I said. "Maybe there's another way."

"I want to help, I really do, and if you can think of something that won't involve thievery, let me know. But until then, I just can't be part of it no matter what good may come of it."

That night, I tossed and turned in restless sleep as I racked my brain. How, without stealing the stone, could we prove it really was the twelfth stone? Then it came to me. We really didn't need to steal the stone, all we needed to do was prove it had the inscription on it. We'd then have the proof we needed. Rosa would still take the lead, but she wouldn't have to step over her principled line. The task needed to be quick and uncomplicated yet evidence sufficient. I needed to think this through very carefully.

***

"Have the camera?"

Rosa patted her large leather tote. "Right here."

"And the paper and pencil?"

"Also right here." Rosa lifted the items from her bag and showed them to me. "And I remember the signal."

"Meyer is at his office so that will keep him occupied while you visit with Mary Anne. I will be back to pick you up at three. When I return, be ready to execute the plan. You'll need to make sure you get the necessary evidence, but don't be too long. You won't want Mary Anne to get suspicious."

"I've got it," said Rosa taking a deep breath and letting it out slowly.

I leaned over and kissed her on the cheek. "This will all be over soon and we'll have what we need."

"I just hope I can pull this off."

Rosa got out of the car, walked to the Belinsky's door and rang the bell. When the door opened, Rosa exchanged kisses with Mary Anne and with a final wave to me went inside. Now all I had to do was keep myself occupied until it was time to pick her up.

I returned to the Belinsky's right on time. Mary Anne opened the door and ushered me into the sun room where she and Rosa had been visiting.

"Ready to go?" I asked Rosa.

"Sure," she said. "But first, let me visit the lady's room."

"Down the hall on your right," said Mary Anne.

While Rosa was gone, Mary Anne and I chit chatted about local politics and the upcoming election regarding the annexation of Boca West into the City of Boca Raton. It was a lively discussion with pros and cons on both sides. I was hoping to keep her occupied long enough for Rosa to carry out her mission. Just as it seemed the conversation was winding down, Meyer walked in.

"Hi Hon. Didn't know you'd be home so early." Mary Anne rose and greeted Meyer with a kiss. I stood.

"Shea." He nodded in my direction but didn't extend his hand. "Where's Rosa?"

"You know women, when there's a washroom close by they'll use it," I said with a shrug.

"Well, excuse me a moment won't you? I need to make a phone call in my study. I'll be right back." Meyer tuned to leave.

A knot formed in the pit of my stomach. Rosa wasn't back yet, and Meyer was on his way to his study. My instincts kicked in—distract him.

"Uh, Mary Anne was just telling me about the upcoming election involving the annexation of Boca West into the City. I'd love to hear your take on it."

Meyer turned around and looked quizzically at me. "I'll tell you when I get back," he said in a firm voice.

I held my breath as my well thought out plan was about to turn into a giant disaster. Just then, Rosa entered the room followed by Meyer.

"There you are," I said with great relief. "Ready to go?"

"Of course," said Rosa. She raised her right hand and scratched her ear, our agreed upon signal that she was unable to obtained all the necessary proof.

"Guess where I found her?" asked Meyer.

My heart sank. I looked at Rosa. She looked at me. I looked at Meyer. He glared at me.

"Oh, Meyer, what kind of a question is that?" said Mary Anne, breaking the tension-filled silence that hung in the air. "She was using the restroom, of course." Mary Anne went to Rosa and hooked her arm. "We must get together again soon, but next time, let's go for lunch at Cheesecake Factory."

"Great idea," said Rosa.

"Well, see you again Professor," I said.

Meyer and Mary Anne followed us out to our car. But just as we were about to get in, Rosa stopped me.

"Oh Shea, I just realized I must have left my bag in the restroom. Would you mind getting it for me?"

I was dumbfounded that she would leave it behind, especially considering what it contained.

"I'll get it for you," said Meyer.

"That's okay," I said. "I'll just be a second." I jogged past Meyer and back inside before he could react. A few moments later, I walked back outside, Rosa's bag slung over my shoulder. As she was already in the car, I put the bag behind the driver's seat.

Rosa waved a friendly goodbye to Mary Anne. Meyer stood on the sidewalk behind his wife, displaying taught lips and a narrow stare.

When we arrived home, I went to retrieve Rosa's bag from the back seat. As I bent in, grabbed the handles and pulled, excruciating pain shot up my back and froze me in a bent position.

"Rosa!" I exclaimed in a mixture of surprise and anguish. I clung to the door on one side and the back seat on the other.

Rosa rushed around the car, took one look at me and knew what happened. My back had gone out, the muscles tightening like a rope being twisted in a vice.

"Oh, Shea, here, let me get you inside."

Leaning on Rosa, I hobbled back to the house, each step swathed in unbearable agony. In the bedroom, I immediately became prone. Rosa rushed to the medicine cabinet and returned with a glass of water, my prescribed muscle relaxer and pain capsule. I'd had these episodes before, but it had been a year since I'd even had a twinge of back pain. Now it was full throttle.

"Here, take these," said Rosa.

I could barely breathe, move, or speak.

"How in the world did this happen? My bag isn't that heavy," said Rosa.

"I thought you knew," I gasped. "It's the stone."

"The stone!" Rosa said in utter astonishment.

I raised my head to speak but the mere act sent another round of piercing torture surging through me. I let out a pain-filled wail and lay on the bed taking deep breaths, trying to relax and praying for relief. Thankfully, thirty minutes later the pain pill and muscle relaxer kicked in and sent me to la la land.

When I awoke hours later, the pain was more tolerable; yet, I had to visit the bathroom and knew moving into and out of a sitting position and lifting my legs to walk would be crippling. With great difficulty and intense pain, Rosa helped me up. Leaning on her, I made it across the room, into the loo, and back into bed.

"Where's the stone?" I asked.

"It's here. It's safe," said Rosa.

"Leaving your bag in the bathroom was brilliant of you. It gave me the perfect opportunity to get the stone out of the house undetected."

Rosa looked quizzically at me. "Why Shea, whatever do you mean?"

"What do I mean? Didn't you leave your bag in the bathroom on purpose?"

"Now why would I do something like that?" Her tone reflected a patronizing tenor.

"Because you wanted me to—"

"Shush," said Rosa, planting a kiss on my cheek. "You need to rest. We'll talk about this later." She turned and walked out of the room leaving me perplexed. Had she or had she not deliberately left her tote in the bathroom so I could use it to steal the stone?

In the morning I was famished, having gone to bed without anything to eat. Rosa helped me hobble to the breakfast table, and though I was unable to straighten up, I did manage to sit down long enough to consume a hefty breakfast of bacon and eggs and swallow another muscle relaxer and pain pill.

"Oh, I meant to tell you," said Rosa sitting down in the chair across from me. "Meyer called last night. Said he wanted to speak to you."

"What did you tell him?" I was sure by then he had noticed the stone's absence and surmised what had happened.

"That you pulled your back out and were down for the count."

"Did he say anything else?"

"No, but I could tell he seemed most anxious to speak with you."

"No doubt," I said. "By the way, you didn't tell me, did the stone have the markings?"

"I really couldn't tell, Shea. I thought I saw something, but it was so faint and the light so poor I presumed the rubbing would reveal anything that was there."

"Let me see the photos and the rubbing. Then we need to take a look at the stone. Can you bring it in here along with a flashlight and magnifying glass?"

"Shea, this is hardly the time. You can barely move."

"I know, but we need to find out if it's really the twelfth stone."

"Fine. But we'll get you back into bed first. Then I'll bring the stone in."

After settling back into bed, Rosa rolled in a cart with the requested hardware; but, the pièce de résistance was the stone placed front and center on the cart. Knowing that this piece of granite might be the twelfth stone and key to the Exodus of the Israelites was a spine tingling experience. Then again, this ancient artifact had already given me one spine tingling and debilitating experience. I hoped the next one would be a bit more positive.

I inspected the photos Rosa took in Belinsky's study and the rubbing she did on the paper. The photos weren't convincing even though I could see some light indications of a possible inscription. As for the rubbing, Rosa had only been able to do a partial rubbing so it didn't reveal anything conclusive either.

"Here, take the flashlight and shine it on the area you believe you saw the inscription. If you can't see anything by shining the light directly on the area, angle the light across the stone. Shadows caused by the indentations from the inscription should show up better. Then take the magnifying glass and let me know what you see."

We turned off the overhead lights and closed the blinds and door. In the glow of the flashlight with not even a breath of air moving, I watched Rosa inspect the stone from numerous angles and distances and tried to observe her face for any sign of discovery. How I envied her. I'd have given anything to be the one to examine the stone, but trying to stand and bend in order to do so was out of the question.

"Well?" I finally asked with mixed emotions, hoping for the best but preparing for the worst.

Her smile lit up the room.

During my ten days of recuperation, I examined the stone innumerable times. I even had Stella use her contacts with the Photoshop boys to embellish the faint images of the inscription on the photos. With their help, the inscription could be seen quite plainly.

Also, while recovering, I thought long and hard about Mort, Misha, Meyer, Helen, the stone, the temple deaths and how they all fit together. All I presently knew is that the stone in the mausoleum was, in fact, the twelfth stone and that Mort knew about it. So did Belinsky. But how? There were still lots of questions and few answers.

I hadn't heard from Misha in quite a while and needed to inform him of the good news, despite the fact that I still held on to my resentment at his refusal to return my rock from Jabal al Lawz. But his stone took precedent. It was far more important than my small rock, and I needed to return the precious relic to its rightful place among the other eleven stones in the Israeli museum.

For that, I needed a reputable company that could get the stone covertly out of the U.S. and into Israel without asking questions.

***

"Everything Middle Eastern," announced the soft female voice at the other end of the line.

"Omar Shama, please," I said.

"I'm sorry sir, but you have the wrong number."

Rather than off putting, her answer was routine whenever I contacted Omar. I hung up and waited.

"Shea, so good to hear from you. Needing our services?" Omar had returned my call in less than a minute.

"Yes," I said, hating to admit that I would be involved with this clandestine group once more. "I need to send something to Israel."

"I'm assuming this object needs to be handled very discretely?"

"It does."

"Everything Middle Eastern would be glad to help. We have a plane leaving next week. A direct flight from the Fort Lauderdale Airport."

"That would be fine."

"There is one small thing I need to mention. On flights such as these, when the shipment is so sensitive, we require the sender to go along to verify that the cargo gets to its final destination safely."

"I would have expected nothing less from The Consigned," I said.

"I will email you forms needed for the cargo manifest and directions to the transport area. If you have any questions after reviewing the documents, feel free to give me a call."

"Will do."

With that arranged, I would wait until I got the information from Omar before contacting Misha to let him know when I and his stone would arrive. I could only imagine his elation at the news. I also needed to speak to Detective Warren. It was time to turn over all our notes on the mystery of the deaths of the temple members and let him take it from here. My plans were falling into place, but there was one small but very important detail I needed to attend to. I needed to tell Rosa I was going to Israel . . . again. I wondered if I should just go ahead and move my things into the guest room now.

Rosa was not thrilled that I was going back to Israel, yet she understood why I had to go. The fact that she had been part of the reason I now had the stone made it easier for her to consent to the journey. It would be short, only four days, with no side road trips—go to Israel, return the stone to the museum, get back on the plane. That's all I would do, I promised. So far, so good. And the best part of all—the guest room was still vacant.

Chapter 22

On Tuesday, I phoned Warren and made an appointment for us to meet at 1:30 p.m. at Sal's restaurant. That way we could grab a late lunch and talk about the suspected temple murders. I had reserved a back corner booth ahead of time so we could have a lengthy quiet conversation.

Warren stared at my nose, taking the liberty to view it from a variety of angles.

"It doesn't look too bad, considering. It could have looked a lot more . . . crooked." He let out a muted laugh behind his smiling lips.

"A little joke at my expense?" I was sure he was looking for a 90 degree angle.

"Well, I must say that you're an easy target given all the things that have happened to you. Writing is supposed to be a benign profession. Ever think of finding another line of work?" Warren perused the menu, then we both ordered.

"Look, Detective, I don't go looking for these stories; they find me."

"I think I've heard those lines before, Baker. Yep, I think it was when I rescued you from the alligators and pythons when your car flew into the C-51 Canal in Palm Beach a couple years back. Remember that? It was during the Spear of Destiny case. It was night. You were standing on the side of the road in your soaked skivvies, the ones with the red hearts and cupids with their little bows and arrows. Yep, I think that's where I heard you say those words." Warren grinned and then let out a vigorous laugh.

"This is serious, people are getting killed."

Warren's eyebrows shot up. "So now Mort's murder has morphed into multiple homicides?"

"If you'll let me explain, you'll see just how serious this is."

Our lunch arrived and Warren eyeballed me as he munched on his meatball sub.

"It started with Mort's murder," I said. I laid out the whole story—about meeting Helen at Mort's funeral and what she had told me about too many temple members dying, the men who had financed the building of the mausoleum, and the research Stella and I had done on purchases in the mausoleum. I spread the documents before him and explained each one. When I was through, he had stepped out of his jokester persona and back into his detective role.

"You do know what you're saying don't you?"

"I do."

"You're suggesting that certain people in the temple are killing off their members so they can recoup their investment."

"That's about the size of it, with one exception. I don't have a clue who the killers are. That's where you'll have to actually earn your salary. I'm tied up trying to prove history."

Warren sat back. "What does that mean?"

"It means I'm on my way back to Israel."

"Another mystery wrapped in scripture?"

"Something like that," I said.

"Look, Baker," said Warren leaning in and shaking his thick index finger at me, "if you're already eyeball deep in this multiple homicide temple thing, you need to stick around while I check out your research and assumptions. And rest assured I'll be discussing this with Sheriff Berry and the Boca Raton Police."

"I can't postpone my trip, and unless I'm under arrest, Detective, I'm leaving Thursday. I'll be gone a few days."

"Does Rosa know about this?"

"Yes, everything."

"Sure she does," he said in a smug tone. "Just like she knew about the last mystery and the one before that." He rolled his eyes in disbelief and leaned back against the booth.

"We've gotten beyond those."

Warren leaned in once again and narrowed his eyes. A stern look came over his face.

"Baker, I know you're up to something, and I know it probably has to do with Mort's murder. You're not the kind to let that one go so easily. What is it you're not telling me?"

I opened my mouth to answer, but thought better of it.

"Not talking? Well, let me tell you something, if you go and get yourself into trouble, there won't be anyone to protect or rescue you over there. And I don't want to be the one who has tell Rosa that her husband isn't coming home."

"It's not like that," I said. "This trip is simply a quick in and out."

"How come I don't believe you?" Warren abruptly rose, gathered the files and left, leaving me with his bill and deep suspicion.

**

Early Thursday morning I met Omar at International Air, a small private cargo and passenger carrier that operated out of a terminal at the Fort Lauderdale-Hollywood

International Airport. Customs had already approved my papers and I was ushered into a comfortable but small waiting room while the rest of the cargo was loaded onto the bizjet. My precious freight was packed carefully in my large carry on along with my clothes and personal essentials. I also carried my notebook computer. My plan was to remain attached at the hip to both items for the duration of the trip.

Omar busied himself elsewhere while I sat in a plush leather seat and enjoyed a complimentary copy of USA Today along with a cup of coffee.

"Going somewhere?"

I looked up surprised to see a tall man standing in front of me. His deep voice, steel blue eyes and grey crew cut were all too familiar.

"Sheriff Berry," I said with a nod. "Going my way?" He wore street clothes and gripped a brown duffle bag in his hand.

"Let's just call it an unexpected interlude from my job," he said pleasantly enough.

"I guess that really means you're planning on being my body guard again."

"Right," he said taking a seat next to me. "It'll be like old times."

"But how did you—? Ah, Detective Warren. I should have guessed he was the informer."

"Detective Warren is a good man. He knows when to apprise me of certain things."

"I'm sure he does. And just what did he tell you?"

"That I needed to keep an eye on you. That you are trying to solve Mort Saul's murder and save the world at the same time. Knowing him, and you, I know it isn't far from the truth."

I smiled. "I guess there's nothing I can do to change your mind."

"Nope."

"Tell me, Sheriff, how do you just take off from your job to fly thousands of miles around the globe just to make sure I'm safe?"

"It isn't just you."

"No? Then what is it?"

I watched Berry's eyes fall onto my carry on. A shiver ran up my spine.

"How'd you know?"

"I have my ways."

"Does Warren know?"

"No, not about the stone. He simply believes, and rightly so, that you're up to something."

I sat there in silence wondering just how much Berry knew.

"You do realize you've committed grand theft and are about to transport stolen goods out of the country. That's a big time felony. Carries a hefty fine and maximum sentence of ten years."

His words hit me like a sledge hammer. For the first time, I realized I had been so caught up in trying to solve the mystery of Mort's death and discover the whereabouts of the twelfth stone that I never even considered the legal implications of what I'd done or was about to do. Sure, Belinsky stole the stone from the mausoleum, but I stole the stone from him. I was just as much of a thief as he was, and regardless of how altruistic my intentions, the stone actually belonged to the temple. A large lump formed in my throat.

"Are you planning to arrest me?" My mouth was so dry I could barely utter the words.

"That would be the normal response to such a crime."

"But how did you even know about the stone, let alone that I had it?"

"Perhaps you need to speak to our host."

"Ah, I see you are getting reacquainted," said Omar walking toward us. "The plane is ready and all cargo is aboard. This way, gentlemen." He turned toward a door that led to the tarmac.

"Wait a minute, Omar," I said grabbing his arm and detaining him. "I'd like some answers."

"Now is not the time," he said, looking down at my hand. "Now if you will follow me."

"What's going on here?" I said, looking at Berry.

"Now is not the time," Berry repeated.

I dropped my hand and followed Omar and Berry through the exit, up the movable ramp and onto the plane. It was a plush corporate jet, the kind a successful company would own or charter for a business trip. It had about twenty seats with a small lounge area and galley in the rear of the plane. Being on this plane and knowing Omar was involved reminded me of our first adventure when we dealt with the cloak. That was a long time ago and I hoped this trip turned out to be a lot less traumatic than that one.

"Your seats, gentlemen." Omar motioned toward a row in the center of the plane. "And this is Ruma. She'll be your flight attendant. Please feel free to avail yourself of our hospitality." Omar turned, walked toward the front of the plane and disembarked.

A dark olive-skinned woman dressed in a blue and white flight attendant's uniform walked toward us from the back of the plane.

"We'll be leaving soon. Please have a seat and buckle your seat belts," she said in a distinct Middle-Eastern accent.

"We're the only passengers?" I moved to the window seat on right side of the plane.

"It's a special flight," she said with a smile.

I looked at Berry. He, too, had a grin on his face.

"I don't suppose you'd like to let me in on this?"

"In due time," said Berry, slipping into the widow seat on the opposite side of the plane. Two isle seats remained between us.

I wondered what connection he had to all of this. Sure, I knew he said he was acting as my body guard, but the last time he did that I was kidnapped at the Western Wall in Jerusalem, the abduction being a means to an end that proved most harrowing. I wanted to speak to Berry, but just after takeoff the law man reclined his seat to an almost bed-like position and dozed off. He let out a light steady snore as though he hadn't had a good sleep in ages. Ruma woke him for meals during which we had brief conversations. Other than that, our catching up just didn't happen.

I slept as well, listened to music, and typed in my notebook. I also sent out a number of text messages. The first went to Rosa. I let her know Berry was on board and that I was in good hands. She responded with great relief. The next one was sent to Stella. I asked her to phone Helen and let her know Detective Warren would be contacting her regarding the temple deaths. The last text went to Misha to inform him that I and the stone would see him at the museum inside twenty-four hours. He, of course, was elated and said he'd have everything ready at the museum for us, whatever that meant.

The flight took us thirteen hours and we landed in Tel Aviv wide awake after sleeping on the plane. A taxi took us to Jerusalem where our accommodations, adjacent rooms, were at the same hotel Rosa and I had stayed in during our recent time there. It felt familiar, and it was nice to be recognized as the real Shea Baker, instead of the grotesque creature I had become after my earlier assault in the desert.

"I'm sure you won't want to let your cargo out of your sight, so I suggest you order dinner from room service and stay in your room," Berry said in a low voice when we arrived at our suites on the tenth floor. His tone and message smacked of being more of an order than a suggestion.

"Why don't you join me? We could catch up."

"Can't. I need to see some old friends." Berry waited until I went inside and locked the door.

From my past experience with Berry in the cloak adventure, I knew that he had more than a few contacts in Israel. He had, after all, been here several times before. In 2001, after the terrorist attacks on the Twin Towers on 9/11, the world learned that the terrorists had actually lived in Florida and learned to fly planes at several South Florida airports. To assist in combating further terrorist activity in the Sunshine state, he, along with a number of sheriffs in high profile counties throughout Florida, had been sent to Israel to attend several weeks of anti-terrorist training. It had been taught by the world's most elite Israeli commandos, intelligence officers, and IT specialists who dealt with both physical and cyber terrorism on a daily basis. He had brought the training back to Palm Beach and remained in close contact with many of the Israelis he had met, both military and civilian.

After watching TV, reading two magazines, having a conversation with Rosa and Stella, and typing on my notebook, I was still wide awake and going stir crazy. It was 10 p.m. and the gift shop didn't close until eleven. I decided to venture down there and take a peek. Maybe I could find an appropriate gift for Rosa.

Knowing I couldn't leave the stone behind, I slipped it into a smaller heavy duty leather bag and slung it over my shoulder. It was heavy, but I figured no one would notice my slight lean to one side at this late hour. All seemed fine until I stepped into the elevator. Just before the doors closed, a hand slipped in between them. When the doors reopened, a dark complexioned man in street clothes stepped in.

"Floor?" I asked.

He looked at the elevator buttons; "L" was the only one lit.

"Lobby," he said.

As the elevator began its descent, it dawned on me that I hadn't seen this man waiting for the elevator on the tenth floor or even coming down the hall. With the corridor quite long, it seemed practically impossible that I would have missed him. As I pondered this, the hairs on the back of my neck suddenly stood upright and my skin began to tingle as though an ominous cloud hung over me. The elevator was now down to the fifth floor; however, waiting for the doors to open onto the lobby was agonizing.

With caution in mind, I pulled my bag close and stepped back toward the rear of the elevator, keeping my eyes on the man. As I did, he stepped back as well, staying even with me. Again, I stepped back, now almost to the corner. The man turned, looked at me and smiled. White teeth sparkled behind a sinister grin and midnight eyes.

It happened fast—a knife blade thrust at my stomach coupled with a simultaneous elbow to my chin. Pain shot through me and fireworks lit up my brain as my head bounced off the back wall of the elevator. Through shock and fog as thick as a blanket, I felt myself slump to the floor. The elevator bumped to a stop and I heard the ding of the doors getting ready to open. As soon as they did, the man rushed out. I remained in the elevator, dazed and sprawled on the floor in the corner. Looking down through unfocused eyes, I saw blood covering my clothes and a bloody knife on the floor.

"Call 101," I heard someone yell. Several hotel employees and guests rushed over and poked their heads into the elevator. Somebody knelt beside me.

"Stay still. I'm Dr. Siegel. I'm going to examine you."

"What about my bag?" I said, my head spinning and my words slurred.

"Let's not worry about that now, let's see what injuries you may have."

"But I need to know about my bag? Is it safe?"

"Please, I need to examine you. The bag will have to wait." The doctor unzipped my pants and pulled up my bloody shirt. He poked around a while then pulled out a small flashlight and checked my eyes, my pulse and felt my head. All the while, curious onlookers gawked at me.

"Move back. Let me in." Berry's voice resonated somewhere in the background as he forced his way into the elevator. "He's my traveling companion. What happened?"

"He was assaulted," said the doctor. "Apparently the blood isn't his; probably belongs to the attacker. He's dazed, but other than an abrasion on his chin, lump on the head and slight concussion, he should be fine. He'll experience a headache and perhaps nausea, but a couple of aspirin, bed rest, and plenty of fluids should do the trick. However, I would recommend that he be examined by his family doctor to make sure there are no residual effects. He was very fortunate. It could have been a lot worse."

Amid loud whales from police cars and an ambulance, the lobby filled with uniformed men. Berry took charge and spoke to the police, while the ambulance attendants placed me on a gurney. The police removed my bloody clothes and put them in a plastic bag to become part of the evidence. The paramedics performed their examination and after consulting with the doctor agreed to release me. The hotel's night manager commandeered a wheelchair, and I left wrapped in a sheet the medics gave me. The police remained behind to examine the crime scene and collect further evidence.

Berry pushed me back to the room followed by the night manager who apologized profusely and said if we needed anything to just ask. Berry assisted me into bed, brought me ice for the knot on my head, a glass of water and acetaminophen for my throbbing headache.

"You just can't stay out of trouble can you Baker?" The tone of his question added to my headache.

My words were delivered slow and deliberate. "Trouble? I told you before, Sheriff, I don't go looking for it; somehow it just finds me."

"That it does," he said.

"What about the bag? The stone?"

"We'll talk about that tomorrow. You need to rest now." He sat in a chair across the room and stared at me. After a few minutes, I went out like a light.

Chapter 23

"Feeling better?" Berry sat in the same chair I'd seen him in last night.

"Too early to tell," I said, rubbing the sleep from my eyes. "How long have you been here?"

"All night."

Suddenly, I shot upright. My heart began to pound.

"My bag!" I exclaimed, having just remembered it. My eyes darted around the room searching every corner.

From next to his chair, Berry picked up my leather bag and dangled it from his fingers. It contained a long slit from which the stone could have easily been removed. My heart sank along with my countenance. I crumpled back against the headboard.

"And the stone?"

"It's safe. In fact, you're alive because of it."

"I don't understand." I grabbed a pillow and stuffed it behind me.

"When the perp tried to stab you, his knife went through your bag and hit the stone. In this case, the stone acted like a wall stopping the blade. The abrupt jolt caused the perp's hand to slide down the knife blade, slashing his hand and fingers. That's why there was so much blood."

"He's been caught then?"

"Yes, trying to receive emergency medical care at the hospital. The police have him in custody and are questioning him."

"But how did he know about it? The stone I mean?"

"Maybe he didn't. Maybe he was just some common thief trying to steal from a tourist. We won't really know until the police come by."

I immediately stiffened to an upright position.

"The police! Won't they want the bag and stone for evidence?"

"They would if they knew about them."

"Wait a minute," I said, a revelation just occurring to me. "Wouldn't the police have found both of them at the crime scene and taken them into evidence? How did you wind up with them?"

"Some questions are better left unanswered," Berry said.

I let out a generous sigh of relief. "So you won't turn them over?"

"They can have the bag. It's got the perp's blood on it."

"But won't they want to know why the man assaulted me? What he wanted? What was *in* the bag? Why I wasn't stabbed?"

Berry looked at me and smiled. "You'd better come up with something very clever, Baker."

"Me?"

"Yes, you. It was your bag. You were the one carrying it. Only you knew what was in it."

I leaned back. "I guess that leaves me holding the bag. Literally."

Berry just looked at me and grinned. "A small price to pay for your disobedience."

I dismissed his tone and words that resembled a parent scolding a child.

"We're supposed to meet Misha at the museum at ten," I said.

"Right. Well, we won't be keeping that appointment." Berry rose from his chair. "The police will be here around that time. You'll need to phone Misha and let him know we'll see him in the afternoon. In the meantime, we both need a shower, change of clothes and something to eat. I'll be back in about an hour. Don't get into any trouble while I'm gone."

Berry placed my bag on the chair. He hesitated a moment, looked at me, shook his head and let out a hearty laugh as he walked to the door.

The police came and went. Berry gave them the bag and some story about not realizing we had it until we got back to the room. They asked me the typical questions one would expect in an investigation: What time did I leave the room? What happened in the elevator? Did I recognize the man? Do I know why someone would want to target me? What did I have in the bag?

I answered as best I could but told them it all happened too fast. The concussion, I said, was still bothersome and rendered me much too dazed to remember many of the details.

The perp, they told us, said he had simply been looking for money. The fact that he had not stolen my wallet or other valuables, however, left the police with nothing but a slit leather bag, a confession they didn't believe and a victim with a questionable memory. This time, I was glad to leave someone else holding the bag.

***

As the taxi pulled up in front of the museum, we saw Misha pacing anxiously in front of the entrance. When he saw us exit the taxi, he almost tripped charging down the stairs to reach us. A handful of security guards rushed after him. Misha's assistant Ms. Frankel and a tall suited man that I didn't recognize remained at the top of the stairs.

"You're here! I'm so glad to see you." As in our first meeting, Misha gave me a bear hug. "Is it in there?" he asked, eyeing my carry on.

I nodded.

"Please, let's go into the museum," he said like an excited school boy.

The guards immediately surrounded us. With Misha in the lead, we headed up the stairs.

"Hi, I'm Jeff Keene, Executive Director of the museum," said the tall man in the suit. "We're so glad you made it safely."

Berry and I looked at each other. It was hard for us to keep a straight face considering last night's incident.

"Ted Berry, Sheriff of Palm Beach County, Florida," Berry said. The two shook hands.

"You must be Shea Baker," Keene said, looking at me. "I guess you're the real hero here." He extended his hand and shook mine warmly.

I removed my hat. "I'm not a hero, sir. Just trying to right history."

"Or is that write with a 'w,'" Keene asked, "considering you're a journalist?"

"Very clever," I said. "I guess both are correct."

We all had a good laugh.

"This is Ms. Rhonda Frankel," Keene said. "She's Dr. Reuben's assistant."

"Nice to see you again," I said. Her eyes darted around but never quite found mine and her hand felt limp and clammy. She shook Berry's hand as well. I wondered how he would assess her countenance, considering experienced law enforcement types evaluated people on a daily basis from their body language.

"Please, gentlemen, this way," Keene said.

Once inside, a guard locked the front door and the rest fanned out across the entrance. Keene led us down the same halls I'd been down before with Misha, only he took an unfamiliar turn. Instead of turning right towards the archeologist's office, we turned left. We stopped at a door with the card swiping/voice recognition apparatus, then headed down another long corridor. As we did, I realized Rhonda was close behind me. Too close.

When we arrived at double doors, she leaned in and whispered in my ear.

"I need to speak to you. In private. The men's room is just down the hall." Her voice trembled as she spoke. I nodded slightly.

Keene opened the door and stepped aside. "Gentlemen," he said as he gestured for us to enter.

The room was spacious with a long conference table taking up a majority of the room. Running in a line down the center of the table sat the eleven stones in individual trays; a tray in the middle was vacant. I presumed the absent stone would take up residency there. Seated around the table were several men who stood upon our entering. Two wore military uniforms, two others suits. I was stunned by their presence.

"Leave us now," Keene said to Rhonda. She nodded politely and closed the door, but not before I caught her gaze and a flip of her head toward the men's room.

"Would someone like to tell me what's going on here?" I looked across the table from one unfamiliar face to another.

"Please have a seat," Misha said. "All will become clear."

Berry and I sat side by side. Misha sat on the other side of me and Keene next to Berry. The other men were seated across the table from us. With everyone settled, one of the military men stood.

"I'm General Schwartz, head of tactical support for the Israeli Defense Force. Before I introduce everyone, please turn off all cell phones and place them on the table in front of you."

Each of us complied with the general's instructions, after which he turned to his right.

"This is Colonel Marvin Schlit, also from my office, David Fogel of the State Department, and Mel Scupp, president of the Board of Directors of the museum." At each introduction the men nodded to us. We nodded back. "These men know who you are and I believe you know the others in the room.

"We're here because of the object in your bag, Mr. Baker. Since we don't really know much about it except what Dr. Reuben has told us, and we don't know what the message is, we don't know how the world will react to the unveiling of such prized artifacts. Therefore, we must plan for the worst and hope for the best. A coordinated effort is underway between the museum, State Department, and IDF on the unveiling of these artifacts. Contingency plans for a worst case scenario are being developed and will involve myriad government departments all with one goal in mind—to protect the stones and Israel. If everything goes well, there will be no repercussions from their unveiling. If it doesn't and our enemies desire to refute the finding and try to get their hands on the objects, then we will be prepared militarily. The State Department will coordinate notifying our international partners prior to the unveiling and will field media questions from all countries."

I had been so intent on getting the stone back to Misha that I hadn't thought deep enough about the possible implications of returning the stone, especially how it would be received by the world. Maybe Rabbi Larkin was right. Maybe there were some people that wouldn't be so thrilled to know that the stones existed, the Exodus actually did take place and the Bible is accurate. Maybe the world would be thrown into chaos by the announcement that the stones had been found. And what of their missive?

"Wouldn't it be prudent to find out what the message says before you jump to conclusions?" I asked.

"The message is important," Fogel said, "but just the fact that the stones exist, are back together, and prove the biblical account of the Exodus would be enough for some to take offense. There are always those who want to create problems. We deal with them every day."

"So, what's next?" Misha asked.

"Dr. Reuben, you will examine the stone, perform the necessary tests to verify that it is in fact the twelfth stone. You will also decipher the message. When both are complete, we will reconvene and decide our next steps. In the meantime, consider this discussion top secret. No one mentions the stone or this meeting to anyone outside this room. Future discussions will remain in Israel among top level military commanders and government officials with priority clearance and the need to know. We want to thank Mr. Baker for his cooperation and extend sincere appreciation to him for his efforts to return the stone." Schwartz looked directly at me. "Mr. Baker, Please place the twelfth stone on the tray provided." He motioned to the tray in the center of the table."

My leg began to bounce nervously below the table and my face became as hard as the stone in my carry on.

"That's it?" I asked. "I don't get to know what the message is?" I looked to Berry for support; he seemed unfazed by the directive. I wondered if the men sitting around the table were some of the "friends" he had gone to see last night.

"The stone is our responsibility now," Schwartz said.

I felt a bloom of red crawl up my neck and face.

"Wait a minute," I said, pushing myself from the table and standing. "You can't take the stone from me just like that."

Colonel Schlit rose and rounded the table. He stopped directly behind me.

"We can, and we will," the general said. "The stone belongs to Israel, not you."

Colonel Schlit picked up my carry on and returned to his chair. He placed the bag on the table, unzipped it and removed the stone. After centering it on the tray, he tossed my bag back across the table. I caught it just before it took a nose dive onto the floor.

"No good deed goes unpunished," I said.

"Come on, Baker, it's their stone now. Let's go." Berry rose and grabbed my arm to escort me from the meeting. I jerked it away, grabbed my cellphone, hat and bag and stormed out.

"Simmer down," Berry said, once we were both in the hallway.

"Simmer down?" I jabbed my finger in his face. "I spent a lot of time and went through considerable trouble to put my hands on the stone and get it here, and all they do is dismiss me like a kid who has intruded on an adult conversation. Not to mention that last night I literally took it on the chin because of the stone. Looks like I'm taking it on the chin for a second time." I felt my blood pressure rise to an unhealthy level. "I'm going to the men's room," I said, stomping off.

"Right," Berry called after me. "And while you're there, splash a little cold water on your face. Maybe it will help you cool off!"

I stood over the sink and looked in the mirror. The face staring back had sweat beads covering a deep furrowed brow followed by flushed and blotchy cheeks. I turned on the cold water and splashed it onto my face. I hoped it would tone down my anger and return my sanity. After all, the general was right. The stone did belong to Israel, and I was out of the equation. It hurt. Big time. And, oh, how I longed to know what the inscription said.

"Is that you, Mr. Baker?"

I jumped as Rhoda's timid shaky voice emanated from the stall behind me. I turned to see an "Out of Order" sign taped to the door.

"Rhonda! I totally forgot about meeting you. How long have you been here?" I grabbed some paper towels and wiped my face.

"About twenty minutes. I locked the stall door, sat on the commode and pulled my feet up in case someone came in. Thankfully, no one did."

"Well, you can come out now." I went to the stall door and gave it a tug. It remained locked.

"It's probably safer for me if I talk to you from here, just in case someone comes in."

"Okay," I said. I lifted my phone from my pocket, punched it a few times and leaned against the sink. "What did you want to tell me?"

Rhonda cleared her throat. From inside the stall came her soft distinct words: "I know who killed Mort Saul and why."

With a huge grin plastered to my face, I stepped out of the restroom, enlightened beyond my wildest imagination.

"I thought you'd fallen in. Was about to go looking for you." Berry eyed me up and down. "What's up with you? You look different."

"I'll tell you later," I said.

All of a sudden, the conference room door opened and Misha stepped out.

"Good," he said. "You're still here. I thought Rhonda had already shown you out." His eyes searched the halls for his assistant.

"Haven't seen her," I said.

"Well, here. I believe this is yours." Misha withdrew something from his pants pocket and handed it to me.

I took one wide-eyed look at it and laughed. "My rock! I thought I'd never see it again."

"I keep my promises," Misha said. "I got the stone, you get the rock."

"A fair exchange," I said.

"What's that?" Berry asked, pointing to the plastic bag I held.

"I'm surprised at you, Sheriff. I thought you and Detective Warren knew everything." I placed the bag in my carry on.

"Let me see you to the door," said Misha.

I snugged my hat on my head as though it were a crown and strode down the hall like a king.

Chapter 24

Berry moved to the seat next to me on the return flight. "So tell me, what were you doing so long in the men's room? You went in as hot as a fire cracker and came out like Mr. Cool."

I withdrew my cell phone and thumbed through several icons until I reached my photo gallery.

"This might clear up a few things regarding Mort's murder." I held up my phone so Berry could see it.

"An 'Out of Order Sign' on a commode stall? Well, that certainly clears things up."

"Just listen," I said. I hit the play button for my latest video recording and placed the phone between us on the tray table. While the visual remained a shot of the sign on the stall door, it was the audio that held the Sheriff's attention.

Rhonda clears her throat. She speaks in a soft trembling voice.

"I know who killed Mort Saul and why."

"And just how do you know this?" I ask.

"Because it's my fault." Her voice trails off, then heavy sobs. *"Do you remember when we first met?"* Inhale. *"You saw my name badge and asked me if the 'C' on it was for my middle name"*

"I Remember."

"Well, it isn't. The 'C' is for my maiden name. It's Clark."

Short silence.

"As in Bob Clark, the professor of Jewish History at FAU?" I ask.

"He's my brother." Sobs.

"But how does he fit into Saul's murder?"

"I gave him a printout about the stones. That Dr. Reuben had found eleven and was looking for the twelfth one. I thought it would help him." Nose blow.

"How's that?"

"The university wanted to expand the Jewish Studies department and was planning

to name either my brother or Professor Belinsky as Dean. I thought if I gave the printout to my brother, he could use the information to pressure Professor Belinsky into dropping out of contention, seeing as how the discovery of the stones would not only embarrass him but kill his career."

"So what happened?"

"Belinsky refused. Sniffle. My brother asked me to find something else he could use. That's when I stumbled on the name Mort Saul."

"But how did you know about Mort and his connection to the stone?"

"You have to understand, Mr. Baker. My brother means the world to me. He has worked very hard and is a great teacher. He loves his job and he's loved by his students and faculty. It just wouldn't be right for Professor Belinsky to be Dean, so I was desperate to find something . . . anything . . . to help him. One day I found Dr. Reuben's wallet on his desk. What I did I'm not proud of, but I went through it and found a note. It read—the twelfth stone, Mort Saul, Boca Raton. I told my brother. He told professor Belinsky. Don't you see? Professor Belinsky *killed Mort Saul to get his hands on the stone so the truth about the Exodus wouldn't come out. His death is all because of me!"* Burst of tears and sobs.

"Why didn't you tell the police?"

"I just couldn't. No one would have trusted me and I would have lost my job."

"So why tell me?"

"I just couldn't live with myself any longer. To think that I was the cause of that poor man's death." Sobs.

"You still may lose your job."

"I know, but I'm hoping you might be able to talk to your friend Sheriff Berry. Maybe if confronted, Professor Belinsky would confess and you won't have to involve me or my brother. Sniffles and nose blow.

"I can't promise anything."

"I understand."

When the video ended, Berry looked at me. "What's wrong with you, Baker? Why didn't you tell me this while we were at the museum or at the least while we were still in Israel? I could have questioned her further."

"She had no way of knowing Mort would be killed. Can't you give the poor girl a break?"

Berry's face flushed and he looked at me with his steel blue eyes. "When it comes to murder, we're not in the benevolent business."

Berry picked up his cell phone and placed a call to Detective Warren. After an extended conversation, he told the detective I would be sending a copy of the video.

"Nothing more to be done until we get back to Florida. Let's get some sleep. But Baker, rest assured, you are officially in my dog house." Berry returned to his seat, pressed the recline button and drifted off.

Upon our arrival at the airport, Omar met the plane and walked Berry and me through customs. Once complete, Berry bid me a curt goodbye and said Detective Warren would be in touch.

"Everything delivered safely?" Omar asked.

"Fine," I said as I headed out of the terminal.

"Then All Things Middle Eastern did their job."

"All except for one thing."

"Which was?"

"I wanted to know what the inscription on the stones said."

"Don't let that bother you too much. One never knows what the future holds."

"What does that mean?"

Omar gave me his signature two finger salute. "See you around, Shea."

"What a minute," I called after him, but he kept on walking. I knew he meant what he said. He would see me around again; that's what I was afraid of.

***

It was good to get home—to Rosa, to my own bed, to my tame life. It had been a remarkable trip, but I was exhausted from the intrigue. All I wanted to do was write articles for the magazines, enjoy dinner out with my wife, and drift into my golden years without any more excitement. I knew, however, that there were a number of loose ends and that I would hear from Warren any time. To my surprise, it was several weeks later before I did. We agreed to meet at the mausoleum.

"I hear you had quite the trip," Warren said as we walked past the Cohen Indoor Mausoleum where Mort was interred toward the outdoor mausoleum where he had been murdered.

"That's an understatement," I said.

"Yeah, well thanks to you, we've had our own share of excitement."

"The temple murders?" I was anxious to get an update.

"Turns out the lady's hunch was right."

I stopped in mid stride. "You mean people really were dying to get into the mausoleum?" It was hard to resist using Stella's play on words. Warren ignored the pun.

"We were able to track down several photos of the recent and past funerals and the same man showed up in each."

We passed through the archway into the rotunda and sat on the black marble bench where Mort's body had been found. It gave me an eerie feeling being back at the crime scene; yet, it also seemed an appropriate setting considering the discussion.

"A temple member?" I asked.

"Not only that, he was on the temple visiting committee. He visited the sick and elderly. Does the name Joe Greene ring any bells?"

The name sounded familiar and I searched my mental file cabinet. Then it hit me.

"I sort of met him at Mort's funeral."

"What does 'sort of' mean?"

"I wasn't exactly introduced, but I saw him and was told who he was by Rabbi Larkin."

"The photo you took when you returned here to the mausoleum after Mort's funeral showed a man heading toward the garden. You said he looked familiar. Did you ever figure out who he was?"

"No, but Helen identified the same man in a photo I took at Craig Shapiro's funeral. She said he looked familiar as well, but because the photo was taken at an angle, she couldn't quite put her finger on who he was."

"It was Joe Greene. He was at each of the funerals of temple members where crypts were purchased after death."

"But how is that unusual? He was a temple member. He probably knew all of the deceased."

"It wouldn't be so unusual except he also was the last person to see a majority of them. After looking at their ages and medical histories, most with typical health issues for their age, the ME didn't perform autopsies. Those are only performed when someone dies suddenly and unexpectedly while in apparently good health or when foul play is suspected. These folks all had a history of medical issues. That and their age didn't raise any alarms with the ME. It wasn't until we started putting all the coincidences together that you provided did we realize something was amiss. So we looked further. We found something, too. Something you failed to discover."

"And that was?" Disbelief saturated my words. I knew our research was solid.

"Niches aren't as expensive as the crypts. It's the crypts that bring in the big bucks, especially those in the air conditioned building. All the people that died before purchasing were interred. Not one niche was purchased after death, except in the case of Gertrude Ginsberg. That was because her husband had been cremated, so her family cremated her as well and purchased the niche next to his. But it wasn't just the purchase of one crypt for the deceased. It seemed he targeted the more wealthy members where there would be a residual effect—subsequent purchases for the spouse and family members."

"But what about Craig Shapiro? He wasn't elderly and he drowned in a canal."

"Yes, but he was from a wealthy family. Seems after his son's death, Abe Shapiro bought a family legacy section, a private gated area of crypts just for the family in the air conditioned mausoleum. Quite a substantial purchase. We'll revisit that death as well. The scratch on the fender of Craig's car may have been more than the fender bender they claimed."

"So what's the next move?"

"Disinterment. We feel certain the ME will find something other than natural causes in each death."

Across from us, the Tree of Life, a marble bas relief, jutted from the wall. Its trunk rose from the floor and diverged into multiple branches. Brown marble leaves hung from each branch and displayed the engraved names of deceased loved ones. I wondered how many leaves carried the names of those to be disinterred.

"With all your record gathering and court orders to disinter, Greene's got to know you're getting close."

"He knows," Warren said.

"But what was his motive? He wasn't one of the original investors. He wasn't looking to get his money back."

"True, but we checked his bank records and there was a substantial deposit in cash made after every funeral. We'll follow the money, but it's just a matter of time before we have what we need to arrest him. That won't be the end, of course. It will only open the investigation up further into the conspiracy as others were involved as well. We still have a lot of work to do."

"And to think it all started with Helen."

"There's more news," Warren said.

"About Mort's killer?" This was the news I'd been waiting for.

Warren rose from the bench and stood before me, his feet spread and thumbs tucked into his waist.

"We made an arrest. It'll hit the news tonight."

"So you got the Professor to confess?"

"Yes. He told us everything."

"I guess Professor Belinsky will soon be writing a new book, one that tries to convince people the criminal justice system doesn't exist." I could just envision him sitting in his prison cell writing away.

"What are you talking about, Baker?"

"I'm talking about Professor Belinsky. You arrested him, right?"

"He didn't murder Mort Saul. It was Bob Clark. He's the one we arrested."

A shock wave like a tsunami surged through me. I stood, took off my hat and drew my hands through my hair as I walked around the fountain trying to gather my thoughts.

"You've got it all wrong, Detective. It was Belinsky," I said, replacing my hat.

"No, Baker, you're the one who's got it all wrong. You have to know how to read between the lines like a trained detective. Clark murdered Mort Saul. He'd been trying to get Mort to hand over the stone for weeks, even resorted to following him. The night Mort was supposed to meet you Clark followed him to the mausoleum. When Mort wouldn't tell him where the stone was, he flew into a rage and grabbed the first thing he could find, the bronze vase. You know the rest."

I looked down at the brick floor where Mort's body had been found. The last time I was here I could still see remnant stains. They had now faded in the hot Florida sun.

"But why did he need the stone? All he had to do was wait a few months and let the museum go through with the unveiling. Belinsky would have been ruined."

"Clark couldn't wait that long. The university was about to make their decision on the dean position. He needed Belinsky out of the running and felt if he confronted him with the stone he would realize he was through."

"What about Rhonda?"

"She was in on it with her brother, her soft spoken demeanor a mask for her real intentions. By telling you her sob story, she thought Sheriff Berry would arrest Belinsky and he would be out of the picture for good. She neglected to take into account the astuteness of our Sheriff and detectives. She's been relieved of her position at the museum and will be charged with accessory to murder."

"Well, what about Belinsky's theft of the stone from the mausoleum. Surely he'll be arrested for that."

"The temple isn't pressing charges, especially since the stone is part of a larger picture. And don't forget, Baker, if he's arrested, you will be too."

Somehow, I had shoved my role as a thief back into the recesses of my mind.

"Well, until next time," Warren said. He turned and headed toward the parking lot.

I stood there in silence, staring after him. I wasn't ready to go, at least not yet. I took a deep breath and filled my lungs with warm Florida air laced with a hint of gardenia. Then I walked into the air conditioned mausoleum, removed my hat and selected a small round stone from the basket at the front door. Feeling I owed Mort a final farewell, I walked to his crypt, knelt down and placed the stone on the floor.

Chapter 25

I sat at my desk and stared at my rock from Jabal al Lawz. It held center stage on my book shelf inside a Plexiglas container. How I longed to share its secret and my photos with the rest of the world, but without corroboration by scientists and archeologists who would believe me? Mine was an adventure only I and a select few would ever know about or believe—a leap of faith, according to Powell.

Every day I scoured the museum website looking for the announcement that the twelve stones would be unveiled and proof of the Exodus would finally be revealed. Weeks went by, then months without a word. I finally contacted Misha via Skype.

"Shalom, my friend. It's good to see you. I hope you are well." I said.

"Yes, yes. And you and Rosa?" Misha's head bobbed uncontrollably and I could tell his Parkinson's was progressing despite his positive words.

"We're Fine," I said. "I'm sorry about Rhonda."

"Me, too. She'd been with me for fifteen years. She was good at her job and I liked her."

"I've been looking for news of the unveiling of the stones but haven't seen anything. What's happening?"

"I'm sorry, but I'm not at liberty to say. All information regarding the stones must stay within Israel for security reasons. Just know that the unveiling will not take place."

I was stunned.

"So your thirty-five year search was for nothing? The world won't know that you found the stones or that the Exodus really occurred?"

"Sometimes God has a higher purpose for our efforts. One we cannot see," Misha said. He seemed unconcerned that all his years of hard work would not be recognized or celebrated.

"The inscription . . . were you able to figure it out?"

"Let's just say the message became an impenetrable wall."

"I'm sorry," I said. "I know how much it meant to you."

"Well, it was a great run while it lasted, wasn't it Shea?" Misha displayed a broad smile.

"That it was, Misha. That it was."

I didn't give our conversation another thought until several days later. Early one morning I opened the front door to find an envelope stuck in it. There was no name on the front, return address or postmark. Inside, a piece of plain white paper contained the following message:

מגן חומת ,שלך המגן כוח ,שלך' ה אני
שלך האויבים כל נגד.

Recognizing the text as Hebrew, I scanned it and sent it to Rabbi Larkin for translation. I got it back within minutes:

I AM YOUR GOD, YOUR DEFENSE FORCE, A WALL AGAINST ALL YOUR ENEMIES.

Curiously, the Hebrew missive was composed of exactly twelve letters and phrases. Searching my files, I pulled out the partial rubbing Rosa took from the twelfth stone and held it next to the message. Sure enough, the rubbing was identical to the phrase that contained the word "wall" in it.

I thought back to my attack in the elevator. Berry had used the same word when he described how I had remained unscathed and protected by the stone—". . . the stone acted like a wall stopping the blade . . ." And then there was Rabbi Larkin's explanation of what the stones from the Jordan River represented—God's protection. There was too much coincidence here to dismiss. It wasn't until later that night, however, that all the pieces fell into place.

As Rosa and I were watching the PBS News Hour, a most curious report aired along with a cell phone video. It showed Israeli citizens celebrating in the streets—jumping up and down, shouting with joy, hugging each other. The correspondent gave this report:

> *Today Hamas launched several missiles into Israel in their ongoing territorial dispute. Instead of the missiles being taken out by conventional defense weapons, they simply disintegrated once they crossed into Israeli air space.*
>
> *Civilian airplanes and ground vehicles do not seem to be affected by what people are calling an 'invisible shield.' It's a phenomenon no one can explain. Palestinians are baffled, and Israeli authorities aren't talking.*

Amad Muhamad, who lives in the West Bank describes what happened when the missiles came to the Israeli border.

"They simply exploded into tiny pieces and came down like dust. It's like the missiles hit an impenetrable wall."

I sat upright. A flood of familiarity rushed through me as I recalled what Misha had said in our Skype conversation: "Sometimes God has a higher purpose for our efforts. One we cannot see," and "Let's just say the message became an impenetrable wall."

Now that the stones were back together, had they somehow released God's protection? Had they become that impenetrable wall? I needed to make a phone call.

"I guess you've seen the news."

"I've seen it," Berry said.

"And you probably already know what the message on the stones says."

There was deafening silence on Berry's end.

"So no one will ever know that the Exodus is true or learn about the historic significance of the stones?" I asked.

"I'm sure wherever they are they are serving God's purpose," he said.

"So that's it? We'll never really know the whole story or how the Israelis discovered the protective power of the stones?"

"That's it until next time," Berry said. "And with you, Baker, there's always a next time."

ABOUT THE AUTHOR

Sally J. Ling, Florida's History Detective, is an author, speaker, and historian. She writes historical nonfiction, specializing in obscure, unusual, or little known stories of Florida history, as well as fiction and biblical mysteries, usually set in Florida.

As a special correspondent, Sally wrote for the *Sun Sentinel* newspaper for four years and was a contributing journalist for *Boca Raton, Gold Coast, Delray Beach, Boca Life, Jupiter, Palm Beacher* and *Deerfield Beach!* magazines.

Based upon her knowledge as well as excerpts from her books, Sally has appeared in two feature-length TV documentaries—"Gangsters," the National Geographic Channel, and "Prohibition and the South Florida Connection," WLRN, Miami. She served as associate producer on the latter production. She has also appeared in and served as production consultant for several short documentaries on South Florida history produced by WLRN, Miami.

Sally has been a repeat guest on South Florida PBS TV and radio stations, guest presenter at the Lifelong Learning Society at Florida Atlantic University and Future Authors of America, and guest speaker at numerous historical societies, libraries, organizations, and schools.

Sally lives with her husband, Chuck, and splits her time between South Florida and western North Carolina.

Sally's books include:
Fiction

- *The Twelfth Stone: A Shea Baker Mystery (Volume 3)*
- *Who Killed Leno and Louise?*
- *The Spear of Destiny: A Shea Baker Mystery (Volume 2)*
- *The Cloak: A Shea Baker Mystery (Volume 1)*
- *The Tree and the Carpenter*
- *Spies, Root Beer and Alligators: Phillip's Great Adventures (Children's Novel)*

Nonfiction

- *Al Capone's Miami: Paradise or Purgatory?*
- *Out of Mind, Out of Sight: A Revealing History of the Florida State Hospital at Chattahoochee and Mental Health Care in Florida*
- *Sailin' on the Stranahan* (commissioned coffee table book)
- *Run the Rum In: South Florida during Prohibition*
- *Small Town, Big Secrets: Inside the Boca Raton Army Airfield during World War II (First and Second editions)*
- *A History of Boca Raton*
- *Fund Raising With Golf*

For information on Sally's current projects, or to become a "Preferred Reader," please visit her website at: *sallyjling.com.*

To engage Sally as a speaker, or to send her an email, contact her at:
info@sallyjling.com

www.ingramcontent.com/pod-product-compliance
Lightning Source LLC
Chambersburg PA
CBHW070859180626
46817CB00003B/837